# THE BOY FROM BUTCHERTOWN

STEVEN TURNER

Printed in the United States of America
Published by: Media Literary Excellence

ISBN: 979-8-89381-127-8 Paperback
ISBN: 979-8-89381-128-5  Hardback

# TABLE OF CONTENTS

# CHAPTER 1
## WHAT IS BUTCHERTOWN?

The old black stem engine chugs down the tracks along Third Street, on its way North towards the "Long Bridge" that crosses Islais Creek. From there it will work its way next to the waterfront and into "The City". The loud whistle sounds several times from the Southern Pacific train that has made its way from Topeka Kansas. The powerful engine has just left the Van Dyke Street Station with the now fifteen unloaded cattle cars. The just recently unloaded cattle will be driven east by a combination of cowboys and Mexican vaqueros along Van Dyke Street. It's a dirt road that leads across the streets that go North and South called Newhall, Mendell, Lane, Keith and Jennings. Between Lane and Jennings are several large holding and feeding pens. Farther up the hill is a wide open pasture for grazing cattle. With in the next week these cattle will be driven North along the five different streets to several of the nine slaughter houses. This area of San Francisco in 1921 is called Butchertown.

There are parts of the twenty six unpaved streets going to the North from Van Dyke to Arthur, that are on Bayview Hill. It has wide open pastures of grass, trees and creeks that over look the South part of the San Francisco Bay. East and down the rolling hills, is Gillman Road that winds along from Innes Street from the North to what is called India Basin, Yosemite Beach, Hunters Point and Candlestick Point. The weather up on the hills is seasonal. It often has early morning fog during the Winter and Spring months. The Summers are pleasant with slight breezes and every once in awhile it can get really, really hot! Candlestick Point juts out from the shore towards the South into the Bay. The winds there are always blowing! And it can get cold at nights. No body goes around it because of its nasty weather! The Point does serve a purpose. It absorbs and blocks most of the winds and cold weather from the areas along the shore going North. Hunters Point, which is just North , takes care of everything else. Yosemite Beach sits in a sheltered cove and is a great place for people to go on hot summer days. It's a well kept secret from those outside of the Bayview District and Butchertown.

As the train picks up speed, it passes by Revere Street and Bayview Grammar School. The school is on the West side of Third Street, which at one time was called Railroad Ave. Third Street at this time, is the only paved road in the area. Almost all of the streets in San Francisco are either paved or have cobble stones. Out in the Bayview and Butchertown, its still dirt and mud when it rains! Bayview Grammar School is the largest school of its kind in the area. There is Burnell Private School off of Oakdale and the three Catholic Schools that round out the educational opportunities before entering high School.

Sitting in Miss Willson's first grade class of eighteen

students wiggles six year old's John Turnbull and Ricardo Landucci. Johnny and Ricardo, who goes by Rico , are part of the class of students from Butchertown. They both live on Galvez Ave and make the fifteen block walk up Newhall almost every morning. Rico walks to Johnny's house from three blocks away and the two best friends leave from there.

Rico lives with his parents, Sergio and Anastasia. They both immigrated from Italy to San Francisco right around the turn of the century. Neither speak any English. They settled in Butchertown after the 1906 earthquake and fire to work in the newly rebuilt slaughter houses. Rico had an older brother, Joseph and his younger sister Valentin. Rico was much shorter than all of the boys in his class He had thick black, short curly hair. With his dark Italian skin, he almost looked African American. He was often mistaken for that and people had a not so nice nick name for him! Along with the dark curly hair, Rico had one thick  eyebrow and dark brown eyes. Although, on the short side, Rico could out run most of the kids, even the older ones. He had a great sense of humor and loved to laugh. More like a giggle.. His body would  often shake as he giggled a high pitched sound! Because no one spoke English at home, he struggled in school. He wasn't the only one though. There were kids that came from families that spoke only German, French, Maltese and Mexican. The Bayview and Butchertown was  a real melting pot of people. All races were accepted and lived together. The people from this area had a special accepting relationship with each other. No one was better than anyone else, they were all the same. Just trying to survive in a new world.

John, as his teacher called him, was known outside of school as Johnny. Sometimes Johnny Turnbull or just Turnbull and some times Rock. He lived three lots down from Third Street in a two story house on Galvez. He had a small area in the upstairs apartment with Lizzy O'Brien, whom he called "Ma" and Rita Behan. Aunt Lizzy as everyone else knew her, was a special lady. Her husband died in a work accident many years ago. She  helps make ends meet by being a seamstress. At fifty years old, she had raised the now twenty one year old Rita since she was six. Rita's parents were killed in the fire after the 1906 earthquake. Rita's mother was Lizzy's sister and was her last remaining relative. Ma took young Johnny in when he was just ten months old. It was going to be only for awhile or until his Uncles decided who would raise him.  Johnny had heard stories about his parents but nothing that he really believed to be true. At six, he didn't understand much. He did know that he had an older sister, Margret! His parents had lost there first child at birth, but he wouldn't find that out until later. Margret had started out living with Uncle William but was past on to her Uncle Charlie and finally to Uncle George Turnbull.

The house on Galvez had survived the earthquake and fire. Mrs. Griffin lived in the downstairs apartment that shared a kitchen, dinning area and a new indoor bathroom. Electricity was installed along with the sewer system during the rebuild of Butchertown after the quake. The city was in the process of putting in paved streets, but that would take a year or two in most places. The backyard was enclosed with an old short gray picket fence. Ma and Mrs. Griffin had put together a rotating garden of vegetables that took care of most of the households food needs. Potatoes, carrots, onions, peas, green beans, cauliflower and zucchini, were what was on the table. There was a horse stable right next door that supplied as much fertilizer as the garden needed. Johnny's father John and his brothers owned a slaughter house on Evens Ave. They had made a agreement to supply  Johnny and Aunt Lizzy what little meat they could eat. Beef liver and beef hearts usually got thrown away, so they always had plenty of that. Beef tongue with the black spots was also supplied for stew. Occasionally, they would drop off some of the better cuts on holidays. Also, Johnny would start working there when he turned six. They could use the cheap labor. Johnny was tall for his age but skinny. He had almost white skin and a freckled  face. His short black hair was parted down the middle. He had two top front teeth with a tiny split to them that you could see when he smiled. That also helped him whistle louder than anyone around. Because Johnny had grown so fast, he was a little clumsily. To watch Johnny and Rico walking together was quite a sight. Two totally different looking little boys that would grow into men and best friends there entire lives.

It didn't take Miss Willson long to know that Johnny and Rico could not sit near each other in the classroom. Those two spent more time thinking about ways to get into trouble than doing there class work. Things like dipping the girls pig tailed hair into the ink wells, bring frogs or tiny mice into the room and poring cups of water on other kids seats were just of the few antics they came up with. They also had a difficult time getting to school when it started or even showing up at all. Neither student had a phone at home and notes from Miss Willson never made it to Ma and Rico's parents couldn't read them. With the summer months just around the corner, the distractions of Butchertown were  just too much. Unfortunately for Johnny, after school whether he went or not, he had to work for a couple of hours each week night at the Uncles business. He didn't dare miss. It happened only one time. Uncle William took a leather belt to Johnny's bottom. So, play time happened on the weekends or before school. The walk to Bayview Grammar School was fifteen blocks of distractions.

On this Friday April morning, instead of walking South on Newhall, they decided to walk North along Third Street. After two blocks they past Taaffe sheep slaughter on Evens and spent some time hanging out at the Dead Horse Rendering Plant which was located behind Taaffes. The guys working there knew the boys on a first name basis. In fact "old Mac" Tilly taught the boys how to "roll there own" tobacco cigarettes. And today, they each enjoyed a smoke from Mac as they sat on the top rail of the corral and watched what was going on. Butchertown had plenty of horses. Way more horses than cars. Third Street was the only paved street at the time.

All other streets were dirt littered with horse droppings. The morning dew from the fog kept the dust down when it didn't rain. When it did rain, it could get real muddy and messy, making it difficult to drive trucks,cars and wagons on the roads.

"Thanks Mac. Rico and I are out of here"

"School is the other way boys!!" Mac chuckled

"Really! Good to know. Johnny and I can hear the Creek calling today. There are a few sea bass with our names on them"

On the short walk of three blocks to Islais Creek the boys passed through Royal Tallow Works on Custer Ave and J.G. Johnson's hog slaughter on Aurtur Ave. Islais Creek is where the original eighteen slaughter houses started. They were built on stilts over the creek in 1868. The cities big wigs had moved the killing of animals from downtown San Francisco to the mud flats and creeks of what is now Butchertown. The creek dumped all of the excess waste from the different slaughter houses into the Bay by using the tide. During the big earthquake, all of the buildings and the pier that were on the stilts crumbled into the creek. So, the business community decided to rebuild on solid ground and not over the creek.

The two boys sat down on the Long Bridge that crossed the creek. They each had fishing line wrapped around a stick in their back pockets. No need for a pole. They put a crude lure at the end of the line and unraveled it into the water. It was about a ten foot drop to the water. The best part of the morning was watching the different types of people and traffic that crossed the bridge. Not having to sit in Miss Willson's class was also a plus.

The school work came too easy for Johnny. Ma had worked on his reading before he started school and Rita helped teach him basic arithmetic.  She was one of the best students at both Bayview Grammar School and Commerce High School. She was also a classmate of Butcher town's favorite son, baseballs "Lefty" Frank O'Doul. Lefty was delivered in a house on Galvez Ave. in1897. Dr. Nellie Null delivered Lefty along with many of the Butchertown kids including John Turnbull.

"I heard Lefty didn't make the Yank's this season. Back in the minors" Rico started the conversation.

Lefty O'Doul had spent the 1919 and 1920 seasons with the New York  Giants professional baseball team.

"That's because he plays for the Giants! He'll get back to the Big Leagues!" Johnny was confident in Lefty and his abilities.

Lefty spent a lot of time in Butchertown during the off seasons. He knew all of the kids by first name. Johnny and Lefty had a pretty good friendship. Lefty would visit the house  during the off season to see Rita. Rita helped Lefty with his taxes and his bank account. Because Johnny didn't have a man living in the house, Lefty showed Johnny some basic boxing techniques. Lefty's father and Johnny's father went way back as kids.

"Got one!!"

Rico pulled up with both hands on the stick to set the hook. Then he started winding the line around the the stick as fast as he could while backing up to get the fish out of the water. It took a minute or so for him to get the fish on the bridge. Johnny got his line out of the way and reached down to grab the flopping bass.

"Bang it!  Bang his head!"

" I know Johnny. I got it".

This technique worked two more times that morning.

Just before the noon hour came around.

"Ah crap! Look who's coming"

Rico pointed North on the bridge to three Mexican boys walking towards them. They were Potrero Hill kids. They usually got along with the Butchertown boys, except Gilberto. He was twelve years old and a lot bigger than most kids. And he was tough. And he hated Johnny Turnbull. Johnny had no idea why. Gilberto had had his way with Johnny several times already and today would not be any different.

"What ya two little girls up too?" Gilberto said as he walked right up to Johnny and looked down into his eyes.

Without blinking , but staring right back into Gilberto's eyes

"I always knew you weren't real smart Bert! Whats it look like?" Johnny wasn't going to back down or show any fear. He knew what was going to happen and it wouldn't be pretty. He thought that he might as well get one good punch in before Gilberto beat the dickens out of him. Johnny landed his one and only swing on the cheek of Gilberto's face.

Diego and Wilmer, who were with Gilberto, grabbed Rico and the three watched the beating that Gilberto would give Johnny.

When Gilberto was done,he grabbed the three fish stringer that the boys had. "Thanks for tonight's dinner! See ya around"

Gilberto and his two friends laughed as they walked back towards Potrero Hill and home.

"You alright Johnny?""Yeah, nothing broke""Your nose is bleeding. It hurt?
"

Johnny spit the blood out of his mouth and wiped his nose with his shirt sleeve.

"What do you think?" Someday, Someday I'll get even with that ass hole."

"What's his problem with you? Gilbert pretty much gets along with everyone but you"

"Not sure"

"You were kind of a smart ass to him today. Weren't you a little afraid?"

" I knew what he was going to do. No matter what I said or did. Hell yeah I was scared. So, I took my best shot before he was ready"

With his eye starting to puff a little and a red face

Johnny said "Old Bert dropped two bits"

He held up the quarter he grabbed while he was down on the wooden bridge during the beating.

Rico started with his little giggle then to a full laugh.

"When Diego and Wilmer were holding me, I picked off a nickel and a dime out of there pockets!"

"Nice work Rico!"

"Lets head to the shrimp farm for some lunch" Both boys started to laugh.

"Yo You Rico, lead the way! We gotta get out of here anyway. Big Dick usually comes by here at noon. If he see's us he'll walk us all the way to school."

They reeled up there line on there sticks and put' em in there back pockets. The lures went in the rolled up cuffs of there pants.

"Big Dick" was Richard Abrams. The Police sergeant  who kept things in order around the whole Bayview and Butchertown. He often road his large reddish orange stallion Scout, so that he could cover more area and faster. At six foot four inches tall and well over two hundred twenty pounds, he and his night stick were a force that you just didn't want to deal with. Big Dick kept his short hair cut from his days in the U.S. Army. His red, almost orange bushy eye brows, beard and mustache matched the color of his horse Scout. The big sergeant always was dressed with his blue cap and three quarter length wool coat. Everyone knew and respected him and he knew and liked almost everyone in Butchertown. Big Dick had a side kick named "Shorty the cop". Shorty stood 5 feet six inches, which was almost a foot shorter than Dick. Shorty had a big barrel chest, a bit of a belly and big round legs. Shorty had also served in the Great War but in the U.S. Marines. Shorty didn't ride a horse, he walked every where. No one knew Shorty's real name, but he to was well respected around the neighborhood. Both Big Dick and Shorty the cop, kept the people safe.

The shrimp farms were run by a little village of Chinese families at the end of Evens Ave. This spot sat right along the edge of the Bay. The farmers used long redwood boats made especially for the mud flats off the ends of Arthur Ave and Davidson Ave. that held the shrimp. They used large triangular nets with an opening towards which ever way the tide was going. This way they would be able to make a catch with the tide  going in or out. Many Butchertown families would go to the village on Sundays after church services to buy the shrimp wrapped in newspaper for twenty five cents. They made great meals for the Sunday picnics.

The walk down Evens from the Long Bridge took awhile. They had to cut through the big hay warehouse on Custer and Mendell and past Bayle and La Coste Fertilizer on Davidson. Next to Bayle and La Coste was a large Chinese duck ranch which extended to the corner of Lane and Evens going towards the Bay. Farther down Evens were the eight big holding pens for the hogs and the California Tallow Works. Butchertown was a very busy and noisy place in 1921. It had nine different slaughter houses. Some killed only hogs while some specialized in the slaughter of lambs. Most processed all three, cattle,hogs and lambs. Then there was the horse rendering plant, a tanner and five tallow plants.

Butchertown was not only known for it's tough laborers and cowboys that worked the industry, but  Butchertown also had it's own aroma! People who didn't live there, but in different parts of the city, referred to it as a smell or odor. Every once in a while some strong winds would blow the "Butchertown Smell" past the Mission District to the downtown area. The Financial District not only got the ocean breeze form the Bay but the  strong smell of Butchertown. The manure from all of the horses, cattle, hogs and sheep mixed with the smells of the tallow works, tanning plant and slaughter houses was Butchertown. It was part of all of the buildings, homes and peoples cloths. San Franciscans only went to Butchertown when they had too! Which was almost never.

By three in the afternoon the boys had made there way back down Evens to Turnbull's Slaughter. Johnny figured he'd go in early today. Usually he would get there by four after going to school all day. Maybe  he could make some extra money in that hour.

"See ya in the morning buddy" Rico had a great time today. Lots of adventures, no school and half a dozen eggs that he bought from the duck farm with the money he snagged from Diego and Wilmer.

Laughing Johnny replied "sure thing! Today was fun".

Working at Turnbull's Slaughter for Johnny's uncles was not easy. It was hard, difficult work for a six year old that didn't really feel welcome. It was part of the arraignment that John Turnbull, and William made when Lizzy O'Brien decided to raise little Johnny in early 1916. John Turnbull would not be able to care for little Johnny and his sister. William who is now fifty one, was just keeping up the Turnbull's end to the deal. John who was the oldest Turnbull boy and Johnny's father,  died in 1918. Johnny's mother, Lilly, passed away when Johnny was nine months old. Johnny's father would pass away soon after. He had heard other stories about his parents, but they were confusing to him. Johnny was to start working when he became six. William had supplied Lizzy with beef livers and beef hearts, which were usually thrown away or sold to the tallow works. Also, he would add some of the cheaper parts of the hogs and lamb that no one wanted. The meat mixed with the vegetables that she grew in the yard made for some great stews.

Johnny started by doing a lot of clean up work. This work included cleaning the new toilet off of the eating area, sweeping and washing the floors and the smelly cigarette butts and spit cans. Coffee pots also had to be washed and ready for the next day. Once he learned the daily tasks, his Uncle Ed who was fifty, began teaching him how to become a butcher. They had given him his first set of old knives. Each knife had a different purpose. He would have to pay for the next set. The brothers paid him extra for butchering. He received twenty five cents for every beef he killed and cut, ten cents for every hog and five cents for a lamb. That went along with the five cents he made each day. Each brother had there specialty, but Johnny would learn how to process all three animals. William and his twenty year old son Joseph, had the beef kill. Ed and his twenty seven year old son Arthur, took care of the hog kill, while George at forty one and Charlie who was forty four manned the lamb kill.

They each had an area where they would kill, shackle, elevate and butcher the animals. They were also the only company that would travel around Bayview to slaughter farmers animals and butcher them. Many people up on Hunters Point Hill and Bayview Hill raised there own animals. Turnbulls did a great job and it was easier and faster for them to do the butchering. Eventually, that part of the business would tail off. In 1929 the Great Depression would arrive. In the years to come after the depression, the homes on the hills would be sold for development.

# CHAPTER 2
## PLAY BALL

Buy 1927, the larger slaughter houses began to buy out the smaller ones. William Turnbull had made a deal to sell Turnbull's to James Allen and his sons. William stayed on with Allens as a salesman. Joseph his son, Edward and his son started working with a new comer, Alpine Packing, who had bought out Rosenburgs. George started with Moffats, which was across the street from Allens on the corner of Third and Evens. With the sale, that left Johnny out of work. Allens had turned Turnbulls into a sausage works. Hot dogs and different types of sausages were becoming popular. They also started to package bacon there.

Being out of work, gave the eleven year old's more time to get into things. Johnny had continued to grow taller. After spending those five years of working, he began to fill out his frame. Those days swinging the three pound sledge hammer to stun the beef, had added some real size to his shoulders, back and arms. Rico also began to grow. He was still a lot shorter than Johnny but he too had begun to fill out.

On this Friday, late in May, school was out for the day and Johnny and Rico still had four hours of daylight to burn. They also had to plan the big weekend ahead. Saturday, they had a baseball double header at Bayview Athletic Field on Jerrold. The 32ed street boys were coming over at 10:00 in the morning and the gang from Potrero Hill would follow at 1:00. Later that evening they were heading to the Bayview Theater to watch a couple of movies.

The corral on Kirkwood was always a great place to spend a few hours. The corral was were people kept there horses. Some of the packing houses, which slaughter houses were now called, always had hogs, sheep and cattle waiting there. The corral also had a fenced off area where local cowboys practiced for the yearly Butchertown Rodeo. Johnny wanted to do better this year than he had done the past two years as a bulldogger. Some called it steer wrestling. Rico had zero interest in that kind of competition but he liked watching and if he could help Johnny practice, he would.

"Two bits says I can beat you to the corral" Rico smiled knowing it would be no contest.

"OK! Here's the deal though. You can't take any short cuts. You have to go down Revere and turn on Lane."

"Your on!" Again Rico still had the advantage.

"Final part of this is, you can't start until I get to Mendell" Johnny and Rico knew some short cuts that would cut the distance in half.

"Nice try partner. It's to long of a run anyway. Lets just walk the short cuts and figure out Saturday."

When they got to the corral, not much was going on. There was a group of younger kids playing marbles by the horses. A couple of the old cowboys were there. "Geno" Dagostini, "BK" (Brad Kudlac) and "Little Willy" ( Chris Wilhelm), were pitch' en shoes  at the opposite end. They weren't to far a way. They usually played for beers at DeNikes Cafe. Even though it was illegal for places to serve alcohol during prohibition, Big Dick looked the other way. Later, when prohibition ended, DeNikes Cafe became DeNikes Tavern. There were also a few horses grazing on what little grass was in the field. Johnny jumped on the top rail of the fence. Rico just leaned on it. Johnny grabbed his bag of tobacco out of his back pocket and rolled up a cigarette.

Holding it out to Rico "you want the first one?"

"Sure. Why not"

Johnny rolled a second one as Rico pulled a wooden match out of his pocket. He put it next to his thumb nail and flicked it by scraping his nail. Not all of the kids smoked, but since old Mac showed them how it was done five years ago, they did. They laughed about Tuesday's adventure. They didn't make it to school but they did make it over to the Albion Brewery on Innes. It had a place where the excess beer was let out of a big pipe that emptied in the sewer. It was out of sight, plus not many knew it was there. This was something the boys would not tell anyone about. They came upon it two years ago while they were poking around looking for something to do. On Tuesday they sat there most of the day catching the beer in a bucket and drinking it. They had a great time!

"That was a good heat on! Hey Rico?"

"Yep" Shaking his head slowly back and forth

"But that head ache later after dinner, was bad"

Johnny agreed" I had one too. Rita got a whiff of me and told me to get upstairs before Ma came in".

Just as they were finishing the smoke, they saw Gilberto, Diego and Wilmer walking down Lane Ave.

"They must have been at "Tortilla Flats".Johnny tilted his head towards the three on coming kids.

Tortilla Flats was the spot where the Mexican Vaqueros hung out at the end of there day. They kept there horses, saddles and hay there.

"You want a leave?" Rico looked at Johnny, knowing that if they stayed, things were probably not going to go good for Johnny..

"No, lets see what old Bert has to say" Johnny had never walked away from a fight and he especially would not run from Gilberto.

"Well look who's here. The little dago and his friend, the no good piece of shit, Johnny Turnbull."

Still sitting on top of the fence "Why don't you just turn around and head back to your place on the Hill."

Gilberto reached down and picked up a small piece of wood and placed it on his left shoulder.

"Any takers?"

During those times when one boy wanted to fight another, he put some wood on his shoulder. When the other went to knock that block of wood off, the fight was on. That's where the sayings "Knock his block off" and " The guy has a chip on his shoulder" came from.

Johnny took the last drag off of the cigarette and flicked the butt at Gilberto, as he hopped off the fence. He had a big smile and his face was red. Rico started to giggle The red face meant that Johnny was mad. By now Johnny stood eye to eye with Gilberto. Which surprised the older Mexican boy.

Without any hesitation, Johnny quickly jabbed at the block

with his right hand and blocked Gilberto's round house, with his left forearm. The red faced Turnbull took a short step back with his right foot as he blocked the punch. Giving himself a good base, he landed his own right to the shocked Gilberto's eye and followed it up with a solid left to the nose. Practicing with Lefty O'Doul was paying dividends.

Diego and Wilmer started at Rico. So, he quickly thought, I'll just tackle Diego and hold on. And he did.

Gilberto started to punch back. They each traded punches and finally went to the ground. The noise the five boys made when they were fighting caught the attention of the three old guys playing horse shoes. They ran over and broke things up. Big Geno pulled Johnny off of Gilberto while BK and Little Willy separated Diego, Wilmer and Rico. Once the dust settled, Geno looked at the five boys and started laughing. Puffy eyes, bloody lips, torn shirts and dirty faces all looked at each other.

"BK! Willy! Looks like we have a little difference of opinion here. What's the beef boys?" Geno stood between Gilberto and Johnny with his big hands holding each boy.

With his face still red. Johnny replied" We were just talking about Saturdays baseball game. That's all."

"That's all ha?" Geno looked at Gilberto. He nodded his head as if to say yes.

"I just might have to come and watch that"

The discussion continued until Geno, BK and Little Willy encouraged the Potrero Hill boys to leave and go home.

The Saturday games were always exciting and fun. People

would come and watch. Some were there to see family. Not too many kids had parents there to watch. There were those who had to work and the visiting teams spectators didn't really want to take the public transportation to and from the games. Butchertown adults and kids always made a good showing at the games on Jerrold.

As nine o'clock rolled around, players from both teams started to gather. Johnny and Rico were playing catch on the home field  third base side. Big LeRoy McDavid, the kids called him Tex, not because he was from the state of Texas, but because he was from Oklahoma! Figure that out! Was playing catch with with Danny "six fingers" Cary. All of the boys from Butchertown had nick names. Johnny was called "Rock" sometimes. He didn't care for it, but it was what it was. Johnny was born with a thicker skull than most. You could hit him in his head or face with a fist and come away hurting. Rico? His nick name came to him because of his short curly black hair and a real dark skin. Negro Rico. He was also sometimes mistaken for being African American.

"Tex" had moved to Butchertown last summer and had quickly become a Butchertown Boy. His father worked at Roth's on the kill floor. He too was a long time butcher. The McDavid family lived on Hudson Ave. between Mendell and Lane. LeRoy was the same age and grade in school as Johnny and Rico. He was a lot bigger weight wise than all of the rest of the boys and he possessed a great personality. And funny!He was always having a good time. Baseball wasn't his game .Marbles is what he excelled at. LeRoy was on the baseball team though. Back up catcher was his spot. Every once in a while he would pinch hit, but he never got behind the plate. LeRoy was the kind of kid who wasn't good at any sport. He did know all of the rules and strategies of all the sports. He also knew the names and statistics of all of the great players.

The forth part of this group that would continue on as best of friends was Danny "Six fingers" Cary. Dan was four months old when the train on Third Street ran over his right hand. He only had a thumb on that hand. Danny's parents were both French and  he attended St. Joan of Arc Catholic Church on LaSalle. Neither spoke very good English but Danny was fluent in French.  Danny lived on Jerrold a block away from the athletic fields. Dan wanted to play baseball, but holding the bat and throwing weren't easy. Danny was the score keeper and went after all of the foul balls on Butchertown's side of the field. All of the kids liked having the young "Six Fingers" around. Danny was three years younger than Johnny, Rico and LeRoy.

Other players for Butchertown included, Team  captain shortstop Ducky Mahoney. He was the oldest and best player. Later on he followed Lefty O'Doul to the minor leagues. He had a few seasons with the Oakland Oaks of the Pacific Coast League. The pitcher and catcher duo was Sean "the Red Rat" Hannon and Mike "Yo " Bishop. He was also called Bish! One would pitch the first game then switch for the second game. Sean was a tall skinny kid with flaming red hair and light skin. He had a decent curve ball  that was never a pitch he could throw for a strike but was difficult to hit. His "Fastball" wasn't really fast, but he could throw it for low strikes. Sean had difficulties at home with his dad. His family, like Johnny's, had immigrated from Ireland in the late 1890's to San Francisco by way of boat. He would eventually move out on his own when he got into high school. Bish received his nick name "Yo" from his love of shooting dice. "Yo Eleven" was his call when he tossed the dice on the come out roll. Mike was a big kid for his age. He thru real hard but didn't have much control. His "Nickle " curve was the only pitch he could throw for a strike. He defiantly intimidated his opponents. Bish actually loved to hit batters. He thought it was funny. Bish was Canadian. Frank, his father, collected the local garbage. John, his older brother worked at Allens as the truck mechanic. He was a Marine in the Great War. No one messed with "Big John". The third pitcher on the team and probably the best of the three, was Jimmy Ross. Smart kid in school. He attended All Hallows, the local catholic school. His father, Wally, was a teacher at a public school downtown. Jim , like Sean, was tall and on the thin side. His best pitch was his fastball. He could locate it easily for strike and he had a great "Knuckle" curve that kept hitters off balance. He would eventually play baseball for the University of San Francisco as a pitcher.

The rest of the line up was, Rich "The Duke" Scrivner in left field. Great arm and number three hitter. He would eventually become a great pitcher at the college level. Mike "The Train" Schaan played right field. Big German kid with a thick accent. In high school Mike would become a force on the football field. Second base was occupied by "Pee Wee" Deloretto. Pee Wee was built like Rico and just as fast. He also loved his Dodgers of Brooklyn. Not a popular thing at that time. His father moved his family to "The City" when Pee Wee as a very little boy. First base was maned by Darrell "The Big Tea Pot" Mehl.  "Tea Pot" was the youngest of all the kids, but was a big, big boy. Probably the best athlete on the team. He would end up playing football at the University of Oregon. After the tenth grade his family moved to little Dallas Oregon. Johnny was at third base. He could knock down any ball. Not afraid to put his face in there and usually did. Rico played centerfield.

The first game went as planned. 32ed Street boys came ready to play. They beat the Butchertown nine five to four the last time they played. This time, the home team scored two in the bottom of the ninth to take the victory. "Rat" pitched the whole game. Bish, clubbed two doubles. The "Duke" and the "Big tea pot" came through with the final two RBI's in the ninth. "Pee wee" and "Ducky" turned several double plays and Rico ran down several fly balls. During the late innings, the boys from Potrero Hill started to show up. As they played catch on the first base side, they began to cheer for the 32ed Street kids. The Butchertown Boys thought that was kinda bush league.

At home plate before game two, Ducky Mahoney went over

the ground rules with Potrero Hills Captain, George "Jorge" Victor.

"The catcher calls balls,strikes, fair and foul. The pitcher has out or safe at any base. 32Ed Street didn't have any problems with these rules nor did Visitation Valley."

"That's not how we play at "The Hill."

"Well, that's how we play here. When we go to "The Hill", we'll use your rules." Duck was getting a little fired up.

"What if we don't like the call" George asked.

"Then you and I will settle it."

"No bat toss?' George asked again.

"Nope! You and I."

"Got it."

Ducky added "Each team supplies two baseballs. You guys have the foul balls off of first base and right field line. We'll take third and left" Ducky was real good at explaining things, while pointing with both hands.

"Danny "Six Fingers" will post the score after each half inning."Danny would use white chalk like the teachers used, to right the numbers on the scoreboard. Big Dick and Shorty the Cop would always be watching the games. They loved baseball, but just in case things got out of hand, they needed to be there.

Being the home team, the Butchertown nine took the field first. Most of the players on both teams wore white tee shirts. Some had the no sleeve look, others had them rolled up. Blue genes, with the bottoms rolled up three to four inches made it better for sliding. A few of the players could a ford steel baseball cleats. The rest just wore there work boots or cowboys boots. Because the Seals were the local Professional team in the Pacific Coast league, kids loved to wear there baseball caps with the SF on them. Most of the rest dawned the pin strips of the Yankees and a couple of Oakland Oaks caps. Pee wee had a Dodger hat. Without uniforms they looked like two rag tag teams, but they could play.

After Ducky relined the base lines, the game began. With Bish on the mound to start the game, it was evident that it would be a low scoring game. He struck out the first two batters on close called third strikes  and Gilberto was out on a questionable out call at first base on a ground ball. Wilmer started the game for Potrero Hill. "The Duke" started things off for Butchertown Boys with a base hit. Rat took a close called third strike. Tea pot was out on a long fly ball to Diego in centerfield and Bish was called out on another close play at first base. It was obvious that all close calls were going to go the way of the team in the field.

"Don't let the count get to two strikes boys, cause the next pitch is going to be  strike three no matter where it is." Duck had a brief talk with his team in the dugout before they hit in the bottom of the third

Portola broke through first with a run in the fifth. George Victor knocked in Gilberto from second base on a base hit to right field with two outs. Before Gilberto rounded third base, he gave Johnny a shove and swore at him on his way to the plate. The bottom of that inning Ducky took Victor out at second base with a cleats high slide. Things were getting pretty intense on the field. Both sides were trash talking back and forth earlier, but the remarks were starting to get personal.

When Pee Wee was called out at first base on his ground ball in the seventh inning, Duck and Victor got nose to nose on the pitchers mound.

"Your rules!" Victor said. "We play by your rules, so get out of here. He's out!"

"You know dam well he beat the throw." Duck put his hand on Victors chest and shoved him while he walked backwards. Potrero added another run in the eight to go up two.

The bottom of the ninth started with The Hill still ahead by a score of two to nothing. In the stands Big Dick and his partner Shorty, were watching. Gilberto was on to pitch the ninth after coming in for Wilmer in the eighth. He needed to get just three more outs and the game would be over. Mike "the train" popped out to third for the first out and Rico grounded out on a ball back to Gilberto. With two down and no body on base Johnny came to the plate. He never struck out and he always swung at the first pitch. Johnny had a nice level swing and liked to ht the ball where it was pitched. Many of the guys were starting to swing with an upper cut because of the Babe. Ruth had changed baseball by hitting so many home runs. In 1919, his first year with the New York Yankees he hit 29. He followed that with 54 and then 59 in 1921. In 1927 the Babe blasted a record 60! It would be nice if Johnny hit a long one, but he wasn't that type of hitter.

"Just get on Rock. We need base runners" Duck told Johnny while clapping and then held up a clinched fist.

Turnbull got in the batters box and as always placed his front foot even with the front of the plate. With his back foot set, he looked out to the mound to see the ball heading right at his face! Johnny jumped back to get out of the way.

"Ball one" the catcher called out.

Johnny thought to himself "That piece of shit. He quick pitched me."

Gilberto was thinking too. "With two outs and no body on, whats the big deal if I hit Turnbull. We still have a two run lead."

With the count one ball and no strikes, Turnbull quickly set his feet and was ready. Gilberto's next pitch was a curve ball, which he started at Turnbull's head. By the way the ball was spinning, Johnny knew it was going to break. It did, but not by much just missing his chin.

"Ball two" The catcher yelled out.

Turnbull stepped out of the batters box. He needed a better grip, so he spit on his hands and rubbed them together. As he took a practice swing, Gilberto yelled at him.

"Lets go! Get in there." He pointed at Johnny.

You could hear the players on The Hill cheering on Gilberto on the mound, and the boys on the home team from the dugout cheering and clapping for Johnny. Big Dick and Shorty split up. Dick went to the end of the fence on the  third base line , while Shorty was down the first base line. It was getting intense on the field. Neither team liked the other.

Without taking his eyes off of the pitcher, Turnbull got set. Gilberto Lopez went into a big wind up and let go of the pitch with a grunt. By far his hardest pitch. Everyone knows that if you really want to hit the batter, you throw for behind his head. Most batters will back into it, instead of going forward. Well that's what Lopez did, and Johnny took the pitch off to the side of his face. At the last second he turned his face so it didn't get him flush. The sound of the ball hitting flesh and bone was load. As the ball bounced off Johnny's face back towards Gilberto, Johnny went down to the ground. Everything went silent for a second or two. Big Dick and Shorty started towards the field. Duck who was coaching at third base was the first to the Rock. Everyone else began to follow him to the plate.

As Johnny got to his knees, Duck asked "You OK Rock?"

Holding his face with his left hand, he reached to the ground and grabbed a hand full of dirt. He tossed it down as he got up on both feet. Looking out at Gilberto, who had a big smile on his face, Johnny's face became a bright red.

"You son of a bitch".

Johnny then sprinted at Gilberto . The Potrero Hill pitcher threw his glove at the charging Turnbull. It hit him but didn't slow him down. He just ran over Gilberto Lopez, knocking both to the ground. Both teams ran to the pitchers mound to break the fight up. Ducky ran into Victor on his way and they started fighting. Rico and Diego were rolling around on the infield dirt. Danny "six fingers' ran as fast as he could and jumped in with Rico, Diego and another Portola kid. He landed some good shots with his stub before he was pulled off by Shorty. The Potrero Hill Boys stayed clear of the "train" and the "big tea pot". Big Dick raced on the field and began separating the boys.

It took a good ten minutes to get things settled and teams separated. There were a lot of torn and dirty shirts. Players from both teams stood holding there hat and gloves in there hands. Some had scratches, bloody noses and lips.

"Na,! That's it." Big Dick yelled out

"Games over. Everybody needs to go home."
"Go on"

Big Dick and Shorty stuck around to make sure the teams stayed apart and then followed the Portola players North on horseback all the way to the Long Bridge and The Creek.

"Nice job guys. We played some pretty good baseball today" Ducky liked to talk after the games with the team. He always pointed out what the guys did good. Duck also tried to say some fun things too. He would also tell them what games he was trying to set up in the future.

"Rock, try using your glove to catch the ball. You stop too many balls with your face. You got so many knots on that head, its hard to remember how you got them !"

By this time the boys had settled down. As they looked at each other, the all laughed at each other.

"I'd love to play those P. Hill boys again at there place. What do you think? We are going to Visitation Valley in two weeks."

They all agreed that they wanted to play P. Hill Then they all had a good laugh again.

LeRoy chipped in. "Hey Ducky,"

"What Tex?"

"I'd pay to see you and Victor go at it."

"Yeah, we all would. I'd like to finish that one too. Rock? You and G. Lopez? What's the  story there? You two have been at each other a few times now."

"Not sure!" Johnny shrugged his shoulders. Then said " All I know is I'll see most of you dopes at the Bayview Theater tonight."

LeRoy blurted out " Lets go get some dinner."

"Can I go with you guys tonight?

"Sure Danny. Rico, Tex and I'll pick you up. Just be ready when we come by."

"Nice job today. Thanks for making things even. I had Diego until that other kid jumped in."

"Any time Rico. Anytime. I was just so pissed off about the whole thing. Then I saw..."

" I know Dan, I know It's all good.' Rico put his Seals cap on and picked up his four-fingered glove.

"Hey Tex, you were a little slow getting on the pile." Johnny laughed.

"Well, I was just eat' en my sandwich when the shit hit the fan. By the time I finished it, everything was over."

Danny took off down the road to his house on Jerrold. Tex, Rico and Johnny began walking down Lane Ave. LeRoy left when they got to Hudson and Johnny and Rico walked to Galvez.

"See ya around 5:00. " Rico waved as he went right to his house, Johnny turned left.

"Sounds good."

By 5:45, the four boys were at Moonys Candy and Ice Cream Parlor. When you walked into Mooney's on the corner of LaSalle and Third, the aroma just changed the way you felt. You were no longer in Butchertown. The sweet smell of the ice cream and candy quickly made you happy. The bell rings on the door when it opens and you immediately see brightly painted walls with happy murals as you walked in. It has a large, long counter with red elevated stools that can turn in a complete circle. The mirror that faces the counter covers it's full length. The framed cherry wood has young children playing carved into it along with hearts and balloons. The booths on the opposite wall are large and comfortable to sit in. Ice cream is served in different sized bowls with thin wooden spoons. Most Fridays, Saturdays and Sundays,  its difficult to get a seat after six o'clock. After a long morning and hot afternoon of baseball. the ice cream would taste so good.

Standing between the counter and booths. "Its to bad Big Dick and Shorty called the game today. We had Johnny on first, with the top of the order coming up." LeRoy took a big spoonful of his double scoop of vanilla.

Sporting a knot on the side of his head and one on his cheek, Johnny smiled and said."I don't think old Bert had any more pitches left in him. I wrenched his shoulder pretty good."

"They didn't have much left to pitch" Tex chipped in. He had watched Portola Hill play several times and knew that they only had two pitchers who were any good.

"The next guy would be fresh meat for the Duke, Pee Wee, Tea Pot and Bishop. That's three runs easy" as Tex continued to eat and talk.

"Lets get going. I'd like to get some good seats in the back." The Rock didn't like people sitting behind him. He wanted to see everyone walk in.

The Bayview Theater was a five block walk up the Third Street hill on the corner of Quesada. It wasn't as nice as the Opera House a few blocks away, but it was certainly good enough for the young Bayview crowd. Tonight's billing included two shows. The first would start at 6:15. "Life of the Party" staring Fatty Arbuckle, was a short silent film lasting forty five minutes. Fatty was the first real star of silent comedies. His popularity had tailed off after a murder scandal that he was involved in. The 1920 film was his best work. Following Fatty's movie was the newest silent comedy hit called "The General." Buster Keaton played a fumbling southern train engineer during the Civil War. Helping him fight the Union soldiers was his beautiful co- star, Marion Mack.

After paying at the little box office outside, each boy took there ticket to the doorman and walked in. There were a few people sitting in the lower-level seats. The upper deck seats would not be available on this night. Shorty the Cop would be sitting there watching the crowd, the movies and probably falling asleep. Shorty looked small standing next to Big Dick. He was very short anyway, but Dick towered over him. Shorty was thick through the chest with a large bulging neck sitting on a set of square shoulders. He was a powerful man.

"Right here." Johnny found the best spot. Middle section last row. From there it was difficult for Shorty to see them. Plus, these four knuckleheads, as Shorty called them, would be able to see everyone in the theater. If someone wanted to look at them, they would have to turn around!

Finally, people started to file in. The Duke walked in with his newest "Duchess." He always had a girlfriend. They sat up front so everyone could see them. Pee Wee was there too. He sat with his girl in the last row, off to the side. He liked those seats because when the lights went out, no one could see them!

Darrell, The Big Tea Pot showed up with Mike "The Train" Schaan and a couple of other Butchertown boys. They sat close to the front and right in the middle. They would be great targets. Johnny, Rico, LeRoy and Danny had several pockets full of peanuts that worked great for tossing at kids. They did eat a few!

Last, just before the first movie started, Bish, Sean and Jimmy waltz in making a lot of noise. Those guys would all go to Commerce High School and be lifelong friends. Trying to find seats together would be difficult. Bish told some of the younger kids to move, so the three could all sit together.

"Sit down up front!" Johnny yelled out as Rico and Tex fired some peanuts at the foursome.

Bish held up his middle finger and yelled out " Yo Eleven"

"Check that out Johnny." Rico pointed to the left as Ducky Mahoney walked down the isle with Marion Turnbull and Margret Turnbull. Margret was Johnny's older sister. "The Turnbull girls are in the house." LeRoy chimed in.

"Yeah, Yeah I see." Johnny didn't sound to thrilled.

Margret being two years older, lived with there Uncle George Turnbull on Oakdale. For some reason the two just didn't get along. In her mind, Johnny was crude and always getting in some kind of trouble with his three buddies. Uncle George did say that Johnny was a great butcher and hard worker for being so young, but he was also" a maverick." He didn't like to follow orders from the Uncles.

Margret went to "All Hallows Catholic School". Which was a

few blocks away from the church. She too, was tall and thin. Where as Johnny could care less about how he dressed and looked, she was just the opposite. Although her clothes were never new, they were well taken care of and clean. Margret wore thick black glasses, but other than that, you could tell Johnny and Margret were brother and sister. Their hair  and skin colors were exactly the same.

Marion Turnbull was Uncle Georges daughter. She was born on the same day as Johnny. February 7 1915. She too went to All Hallows Catholic School.  Marion had long flowing blonde hair. She also had light skin and deep blue eyes. Her walk showed off her slim but full figure. Marion Turnbull was a very attractive girl. Unfortunately for all of the boys, she was head over heels for Ducky Mahoney!

Before the final movie was over, the boys had run out of stuff to throw, got bored and left.

Johnny, Margret and Marion would see each other every Sunday at the Catholic Mass at All Hallows. Johnny and Jim Ross were always the alter servers at that mass. Sometimes they would talk, other times just wave. The whole Turnbull family would also be there. Uncles William, Ed, Charles, Stephen, George and Aunt Mary along with their families. Sundays were a collection of the different families of the neighborhood. The Allen family was always there. This really connected them to the people of Butchertown. The owners of the other big packing hoses lived on the other side of San Francisco. Johnny made sure he said hello to James and his sons Jack and Doug Allen every Sunday.

# CHAPTER 3
## THE ROCK

Johnny walked into DeNikes Cafe on this November Saturday morning. He had been selling newspapers at the corner of Third and Evens every morning for three months. When he took over the route in late August, it wasn't selling many papers. The Chronicle had been San Francisco's morning paper for years. Since Turnbull's Slaughter had closed and Johnny had been out of work, things around the house on Galvez had been getting tight. Johnny felt he needed to chip in, so he got the job of selling papers. Every morning at 5:30 he'd be walking up and down Third Street and down Evens selling the papers. He had to hustle and actually sell the papers. He had started to develop usual costumers because he was there every morning, plus he had a great personality that everyone liked. Johnny made sure he'd walk into every business office at every packing house and sell to all of the store owners on Third Street.. When the number 29 electric car delivered workers for the day, he was there barking out the headlines of the day.

"Hey Cyril. How bout a cup of Mud?"

Johnny liked his coffee very hot. No cream. No sugar. Cyril always showed up early in the mornings on the weekends to serve breakfast. DeNikes Cafe served breakfast only on Saturdays and Sundays until noon. Then it was time to get ready for the dinner and late evening crowd. Monday through Fridays the Cafe opened for the dinner hour at five. Cyril would kick everyone out at one in the morning. Even though the sale of alcohol was illegal, Cyril served anyway. Just no beer. That was hard to come by. Big Dick , as most Cops in the City, could care less. As long as Big Dick or Shorty never had to go into DeNikes because of trouble, they had no problems. Cyril carried a big stick behind the bar and wasn't afraid to use it. The stick was actually an old Irish shillelagh.

Cyril DeNike was a large man. He had been in the business for years working his way up what people thought was the Irish Mob's ladder. The Irish Mob was just big enough in the City to have some political influence. It wasn't as strong as it was early on when San Francisco started out as a city. DeNike was well liked by the neighborhood and supported the local churches. He also contributed to the Bayview Athletic Club and was on the Bayview Stampede Board. The Stamped was the local Rodeo that the coral put on every year. In the later years , the 30's and 40's he would sponsor  local semi pro baseball teams that were very successful. Because Johnny lived next door to the Cafe and the fact the Cyril used to work for Johnny's father when he was young, Cyril took a liking to the young Turnbull.

"Big Dick saw me this morning. He told me to tell you him

and Shorty were com 'en by tonight." Every once in a while the two policeman would pay a visit to DeNike's during the evening. They didn't want people saying that they never checked on Cyril. They'd usually use one of the boys that DeNike trusted and could keep there mouths shut. Cyril would have to spend this afternoon hiding his liquor.

"Thanks Johnny. Coffees on me this morning."

"You going to need some help this afternoon?

"Sure. Why don't you come by at noon. I'll buy you lunch and we can get started."

In 1928, things were going good around the old USA. Ten years after the war saw the country

experiencing the "Roaring 20's. The country was so large it had parts with there own identities. The East coast was way different than the West coast. The South was still segregated and it's own little world. The middle of the country also had its own flavor of life that was different. Oregon,Washington, Idaho, Montana and Utah were out in the wilderness!. Life in San Francisco was booming. Businesses were starting, people were making money and the city was growing in population. San Francisco was the most popular port of call for those traveling buy ship and it was the  first stop for the imports from the Far East. Shipping was a very big business. Freighters transported every thing up and down the coast from Alaska to Hawaii to San Diego.

While Johnny and Cyril ate lunch at the counter together, Johnny began asking questions. Questions about his past and specifically about his family.

"Cyril. Ya know that I really don't know much about my folks. My Uncles are pretty tight lipped about everything and I've never got the real low down about everything. Ma keeps telling me she'll talk about things, but there is always " just no time." So, will you tell me the truth?"

"Johnny. It's not my place to tell you those things. "

"God Dam it Cyril. I'm thirteen years old. It's time I know what happened! Please tell me the truth!"

"It might take awhile, but here is what I know."

"Your dad and his family moved to the City after he was born. They wanted to get away from the Irish Gangs in New York. Your Grandfather was a butcher there and heard they needed butchers out in San Francisco, so they made the move."

"Being the oldest, your dad watched out for all of the younger kids going through school. I think he got tired of that and the responsibilities and wanted some excitement in life. After finishing high school, he went to work over at Moffatt's on the old pilings over the creek. They put him to work on the kill crew. His large frame helped with the swinging of the four pound sledge hammer. Smashing skulls didn't bother him. Some guys just couldn't do that sort of thing."

"Up on the Hill, whats now called Portola Hill, was Irish Hill. It was much larger then. They been using the dirt and rocks of the Hill after the quake to fill in parts of the Bay and build roads."

"The Hill was a poor mans "Barbary Coast." It didn't have the opium dens and the Chinese. Irish and Scots only! Mostly the Irish. Irish mob made sure that the Chinese stayed out."

"It had forty or so wooden boarding houses for all of the single Irish young men. I lived in one of the many shacks and cottages that spread out around five big Hotels. This was all about two miles from here, right off old Railroad Ave."

Cyril paused to take a swing of coffee.

"The Hotels each had about ten to twelve very small rooms with only a bed and a wash basin. They also had very large saloons were there was dancing and some had  large stages for entertainment. All of the women that were there worked there. You had; The Green House, The White House, The Cash Hotel, The Monterey House and Galeys Hotel. These five places supported all of the young guys working at the Mill at the bottom of the Hill. Other guys worked in the ship yards and in Butchertown."

"On Saturday afternoons, outside of Galeys Hotel, They would have Hay Ring fights. Bare knuckles. Guys would fight between a bunch of hay bails formed in a square.. The only guys allowed to fight were guys who worked at one of the hotels, but anyone could watch for a price. Your dad loved to watch those guys fight. Some of them had real reputations and were like hero's. After the afternoon fights, everyone would go over to Boyles Steam Dump and drink steam beer for a nickel a pop."

Johnny's eyes were wide open now and he was taking every word in.

"Some how your old man got a job as a bar back at the Monterey. It was a shit job. I know because that's how I got started and where I started. He was cleaning glasses, floors, puke and sometimes the toilets. He changed the kegs and stocked the liquor shelves. He did all of the shit the bar tenders didn't have time for or didn't want to do. You didn't get paid much, but it sure could get exciting in those places. Loud piano and organ music, drinking, dancing, partying and plenty of painted up women with very little on them. Your dad was old for a bar back.. I was 15 when I got started.

"He got his first fight against a parolee from Galeys Hotel. Your pops was strong as an ox. He'd been swinging that big ole sledge a lot. Plus, he was a lot like you. He couldn't be hurt by a punch to the head or face. It was like hitting solid rock. That's how he got his nick name. The Rock. He beat the shit out of his first couple of guys. No real contest. So, they started to put him up against some of the good ones. It wasn't as  easy for him because they knew how to box. He got better and still kept winning."

Johnny put his hand up signaling to Cyril to stop. He wanted to think about what he was just told.

Cyril went on  when Johnny waved at  him too.

"Jimmy Cole", the owner of the Monterey took a real liking to Rock and made him a full time bartender. Your dads parents didn't like the fact that he was working the second job, fighting and hated those places on the Hill. That's why they came to the City, to get away from those places and that kind of life. Your Grandfather tossed your dad out of the house and forbade him from being a part of the family. It wasn't good."

"Rock" took a room at The Monterey. He was there all of the time, either working or having fun. He made good money . Then Jimmy put him in charge of the whole operation. Your dad wasn't only a tough guy but he was smart and people liked him. He was at ease with telling people what to do. My stick! That was his. He cracked many heads with that when guys got out of line. No one gave him any shit. He was the best in the hay ring by now and people feared him. Every once in a while some  young idiot would test him. Never a pretty thing. Rock took care of the dancing girls, collecting there fees and making sure guys paid the girls. This had become his family now. As his reputation around the area grew, he became more distant from his brothers and parents."

"Jimmy Cole was the rich powerful head of the Irish Mob on the Hill. His well paid enforcer, right hand man was Rock Turnbull. I knew he liked it when he first started, but it does get old. "

"He meet your Uncle Williams wife at there wedding. William had hoped John wouldn't come but he did. At the wedding, he was real polite and didn't cause any problems. He also meet Lillian Lockran. Your mother. She was the younger sister of Williams new wife. Lillian was a real quite lady. Way different than all of the women he was used to being around for the last few years. She was a plain looking gal at first, but if you really looked into her eyes, she was very pretty. They hit it off at the wedding but nothing came from it. Rock had to go back to his world. In 1906 the quake and fire destroyed everything on Irish Hill. It changed things for everyone. I had been working at The Monterey for Rock at the time as a bartender. He took good care of me. Showed me the ropes so to speak."

"After the fire one thing led to another and Rock somehow talked his brothers into starting there own business. Turnbulls Slaughter on Evens. Rock had been saving his money and had the money to buy the land and start the business. He needed partners whom he could trust and the brothers needed the work, so they reluctantly joined in. Rock did all of the business end. The brothers did all of the butchering Rock used his old connections from the Hill to drum up business. He some how knew all of the owners of the butcher shops in Chinatown. Your dad knew how to charm the right people and he worked his ass off and made sure his brothers did too. The business started to do very well."

"Rock started to visit Lillian at her parents farm way out on Quesada. They would spend Sundays at the beach. The Cliff House, Sutro's pools and play land was a place they could get away from Butchertown and have fun. Saturdays they would often take in a show at the Bayview Theater. They had a great time together. They eventually had a very small wedding and lived in that two story white house on Lane just off of Oakdale.. There first baby, a girl, died at birth. Then they had your sister and finally you."

"The owners of the other slaughter houses knew how hard the Turnbulls were working. They did great work and John Turnbull was a real good business man. They were becoming a real threat. Your dad was also one of the local volunteer fireman. He loved driving the team of horses pulling the engine down the streets. Wind in his face and always a fat cigar, he was a hell of a sight."

"OK. What happened to my mother?" Johnny was all ears at this point He wasn't sure yet what to think.

"Well, I'm not really sure, but a little after you were born, she began to have problems."

"What kinda problems?" Johnny asked

"Well, Rock took her up to the State Hospital in Stockton and that's where she stayed until she passed."

Tears began to roll down Johnny's face and he became very quiet. Neither said any thing for a long moment. Finally Johnny asked with a shaky voice,

"Isn't that for crazy people?"

Cyril didn't know how to answer that so he said "That's when Lizzy took you in and Margret went to Charles, I think."

Cyril was now speaking with a very low voice as he could see the look in Johnny's face. Cyril wasn't enjoying this at all. He didn't like hurting the kid. Johnny just stared straight ahead.

"Your dad became very angry He went back to drinking. Fighting. He and his brothers went back to not getting along and even fighting with them. Then one morning, when they came to work, there he was lying on the floor of the office. He died during the night."

"Why didn't my family want me? They took in my sister?" Johnny started to shake his head and said

" This is a lot to take in. I'm not sure what to think about all of this." Johnny whipped the tears off of his cheek and pulled his forearm across his running nose.

Cyril had one last thing that he thought Johnny should know.

"Oh, one other thing. As long as I'm telling you all of this stuff."

"What's that Cyril?What else should I know?"

"Before your parents got together your dad had a girl friend from the Hill."

"So, what's the problem with that? Johnny asked

Cyril replied "She was a Mexican gal named Anita Lopez and she had a little boy."

Johnny turned his head sideways with a question look on his face. Waited a few seconds, then looked at Cyril

"No way! You gotta be shit 'ten me" Johnny yelled out and silently cried as more tears rolled down his face.

"Gilberto? Gilberto is my half brother?" Johnny shook his head.

"Your dad left Anita before he knew. He really wanted to be with Lillian and have a family with her. Not Anita. Rock would give me money to give to her and Gilberto. Your mom never knew, but I think your Uncles did."

"I guess that's why they didn't want me. They always tell me I'm going to be just like my old man. They really didn't like him."

Things got quite again and Johnny asked Cyril " What was he like Cyril, my dad. The truth."

"The Rock was always good to me. A lot of people liked him. He could have a great time. He loved to laugh and be around people. He had something special about him that his brothers didn't have. He loved his family. He was very proud of his wife and his two children. He enjoyed Mass on Sundays. Any time there was a fire in the neighborhood, he was there to help. People were starting to trust him. John Turnbull was a good man, who was trying to make up for his mistakes. "

Johnny looked down at the counter he was sitting at "I can see why Gilberto hates me. Does Ma know all of this?"

"Not sure what she knows Johnny. That's probably why she doesn't want to talk about it. She doesn't know what or how much to tell you."

"Thanks Cyril. A lot to think about ha!"

"Yep. Let's get started on the booze, so you can get out of here and go home."

"Sounds good" as they stood up. "Maybe Ma and I'll find time to night!"

Later that evening, Johnny, Ma and Rita all sat down in the upstairs apartment on Galvez and told each other all that they knew. No more secrets.

Sundays soon came along with opportunities for Johnny. Jack and Dougie Allen had back to back Sunday conversations with Ma about Johnny coming to work for them. By now Butchertown was down to three large packing houses with Allens being the largest. Ma wasn't so sure about John, as she called him, no  longer going to school, so that he could work full time. It took Johnny some convincing but they came to an agreement that he would start after the new year.. He had two months to acquire the night paper route for the S.F. Examiner. He would give Rico his morning business when he started the night route. Things were still tight for Ma, so all the extra work would help.

Johnny really missed his time with his good friends Rico, LeRoy and Dan. The adventures would continue, but they'd have to be on weekends.

Working at Allens was a lot different from his time at Turnbulls. He was paid an hourly wage that could be equal to what everyone else made. He liked the fact that the longer he stayed with the job, he would get pay increases. The kill floor operation was set up as an assembly line , only in reverse . Everyone had one simple job for each of the lamb, hog and beef killed. Leo Federico had been the foreman for years. He watched over his forty three man crew as he walked through them. Marvin Bernhagen was the only guy on the clean up crew. He didn't start with everyone else. He came in later and finished after everyone else. Marv was a middle aged German with a thick accent. Where as most of the workers smoked, Bernie chewed plug tobacco.

The crew was taking there lunch break after they had

completed both the lamb and then the hog kill.  They would move to a different area for the beef kill. This gave Bernie time and room to start his clean up of the new stainless steel lamb and hog kill room.

Leo puffed on his newly lit Cuban cigar. When it burned out, he loved to chew on it. It still gave him a small buzz.

"Well easy money, how's it going. New job and all?" Johnny had been working with the crew for a month.

"Good Leo. I like learning how to do different job's. It certainly isn't boring."

Jack an Dominic Federico were sitting with Leo and Johnny at the lunch table. They were  Leo's younger brothers who had been there for years.

"Your getting faster and better. " Jack said as the cigarette he was smoking bounced up and down. He had to squint his eyes as the smoke rose past them. Jack had a deep voice and was the biggest of the brothers. He didn't like to bull shit people and he didn't like to be bull shitted. He was always brutally honest and straight up. Some guys didn't like that, as he had been in several squabbles in his time.

"You got to be more careful. Do things right all of the time. Leo may not, but if you screw us up and cause us overtime, I'll take your skinny  ass outside. I don't give a dam how young you are. "

" Don't listen to that bald headed blow hard, I got your back Turnbull." Dominic smiled at Jack. Dom was the brother who kept things easy going. He was a true character. Great card player and a pretty good high school athlete.  While holding his smoke in his left hand, between his thumb and second finger. He took a big pull and blew the smoke right at Jack. Then he flicked the ashes with his pointing finger. Jack Stood up and Dom just laughed. "Sit down big boy." They were always at each other.

"When your through being entertained by those two and finished eating, go help Bernie start with the clean up. He'll bitch you out and tell you to get lost. But that's just Hagen! Toss him this." It was a piece of plug chew. Bernie never passed up a free chew.

# CHAPTER FOUR
## LET'S GO TO THE BEACH

Summers in the Bay area are unlike any where else. It very seldom gets too hot. Most days are warm and pleasant. Along the inner Bay and out around the ocean side, the air has a calming effect. You feel happy and it's like you can do anything. The ocean breeze is like having a big fan cooling you off. The only problem with the summers in Butchertown is that the smell never really goes away. It's almost stagnate. Old hide and animal manure gets into your nose and eyes. Every once in a while the people just had to get away. The winter months weren't too bad because the cold was every where. The winds and rains also seemed to cover the odor. When spring came, the grass grew and the flowers began to bloom, peoples spirits began to rise. The young adults looked forward to "getting to the Ocean beach." for a day of fun, relaxation and a different world.

This was early July of 1930. The Great Depression was in full swing. People around the country were struggling to keep jobs. Money was not as easy to get as it had been in the twenties. Butchertown wasn't a rich neighborhood before the stock market crash of October 1929 and it didn't change much during the depression. The packing houses weren't adding jobs and very few people lost them. The production was down but the owners kept the businesses going. Johnny had been with Allens for a year and a half and Rico had gotten on the previous July. Both decided to not go to high school and get started working.

Rico worked in what was called the "Pork Room." In that building, the butchers broke the hogs down into different cuts. They would then package them and get them ready to be sold and delivered. San Francisco had the only packing houses west of Saint Louis. They supplied all of the cities on the west coast and large parts of Texas, Oklahoma, Arizona, New Mexico, the Dakotas along with Idaho,Oregon, Washington  and Utah. The U.S. Military also bought there meats from this area. Much of the meat was placed on trains in ice cars and sent to distribution sites around the country. Local meats were now trucked in ice cooled trailers around town,across the Bay and down the Peninsula. Instead of getting deliveries, butchers and butcher shop owners in the area would also come by and buy what they needed.  Johnny was still working the kill floors and occasionally learning how to grade the beef. Jack and Doug Allen were trying to teach the entire business to Johnny a little at a time. They had plans for him down the road.

On this Saturday morning "the boys" all gathered at the corner of Third and Evens Ave. at 9:30. Danny and LeRoy were waiting peacefully, looking into the windows of DeNikes Cafe as Johnny and Rico walked up. Johnny had been up earlier to help Ma in the garden and then have a couple pieces of bacon, three eggs over easy and a hot cup of black coffee.

They jumped on the number twenty nine electric car for a nickel and headed to Market Street. From there they transferred to the "Market Street Express" to Ocean Boulevard. The ride out to the Pacific Ocean would take twenty or thirty minutes. It started out as an express but things changed. They would make several stops along the way. The Hayes Street hill which was part of the trip was a steep and long part of the trip.

"Whats the first thing you guys want to do when we get there?"

Dan was really  excited. He had never been to the "Beach", but had heard all of the stories about it.

A man named Mr. Whitney had bought "Playland at the Beach" three years ago and renamed it "Whitney's Playland". It sat on ten acres of land along the Great Highway. On the other side of the Highway was Ocean Beach and the Pacific Ocean. At the North end of the beach along the rocks overlooking the Pacific was the famous Cliff House. It contained several famous restaurants and a few bars. This was a popular place for adults to go to. Depending how much money you were willing to spend, dictated which restaurant and bar you went to. The ones that had big glass windows with ocean views or views of Seal Rocks could cost you a pretty penny.

"Lets start off at Sutro's. We can rent a locker for the day to store our shit so that no one will steal it when we ain't using it." Johnny had been here a couple of times before and the first time he had some items stolen when he wasn't looking.

"Then we can hit Playland while it's still cool out."

The day was going to be one of those hot days that didn't happen very often. The walk from Sutro's Bath to Playland, which was located right next to the Cliff House took bout four minutes.

"The Bob Sled Dipper" starts at noon. So, we got at least an hour to check things out. " Rico chuckled. He loved the Dipper. He too had been at Playland before.

"Well, I'm not eating anything before I get on that roller coaster." LeRoy rubbed his belly.

"Smart idea Tex, but can you wait that long?" Johnny pitched in.

LeRoy looked at Johnny and said " Hey Rock buddy, I think I got something for ya." LeRoy reached into his blue genes back pocket and pulled out a fist with the middle finger pointed down.

" If you can't hear it, let me turn the volume up for you !" Tex flipped the fist around so that the middle finger was pointing up.

"Ha! Nice Pal ! Lets go!" Johnny waved his arm towards the fun.

Playland wasn't as busy as it was before the Depression, but Saturdays and Sundays had its biggest crowds. It had several different shooting galleries, baseball throwing booths and concessions every where. The galleries had different types of games were you could win; money, toys, stuffed animals, things that you would give your best girl. Of course, the people working these galleries were always trying to work deals and con people into losing there money. And they were very good at pulling people in.

The rides were plenty to choose from. The roller coaster went from noon until midnight. All other rides started at nine in the morning. Lines were always long for the Ferris Wheel at night, so "the boys" made sure they got on early. Other rides included; The Aeroplane Swing, The Whip, Dodg'em, and the Ship of Joy.. LeRoy would call them"The Puke Rides". "The boys" made sure they rode 'em with empty stomachs.

Playlands's most famous ride for years was called "Shoot the Chutes". It was a ride built in the early 1910's. You had to climb winding wooden stairs to a very high slide. You would then sit on a potato sack. Many couples would sit one in front of the other. When you were ready you'd hold on to the front of the sack and speed down the chute. At the end you would splash through some water and get out.

All around Playland were souvenir shops, a couple of quick photo studios and food vendors on foot. It was a very loud place. Noise from screaming children and adults on the rides, music piped in from large speakers playing piano and organ arraignments, workers barking out invitations to ride there rides, play there games and the mechanical sounds from the rides. It was an exciting place to be. The Pacific Ocean air had its own salty pleasant aroma that added to every thing going on.

"The boys" made sure that they hit every "Puke Ride" before they would jump on the "Dipper" just after noon. Then they would eat some lunch.

"Coney Island Red Hots, Red Hots a dime." called out a gentleman wearing a silver hot box strapped to his chest with steam coming from it. In the box were the famous new craze, hot dogs. He was dressed  in all white; long pants, long sleeve shirt, including a white cap with the Playland insignia on it.

"I got the first round men." Rock called out.

"I'll take five Sir."

"Tex, I'll get ya two. "

"Thanks bud. You the man." Tex replied back. Johnny had a little more money than LeRoy and Dan. They didn't work and even though they saved up for this, they didn't have much. Rico and Johnny took care of there friends when they could.

"Cotton Candy! We got to have some of that." Rico found a concession stand that sold the pink fluffy stuff. He loved its sugary taste.

They found a bench in the middle of Playland along what people called "Midway". That's where everyone walked at some time. It was the main drag or street. Great place to watch people, especially girls. Not that any of these guys would approach one. But it was fun.

After lunch around one, they made there way to Sutro's Bath. Sutro's was something else.  It had six saltwater swimming pools that had fresh ocean water pumped into them. The water was a little cold but really did feel good. It was indoors and surrounded by 100,000 feet of glass and built with 600 tons of steel.

"Oh my God. " Dan said with his eyes wide open.

"Can you believe this place." He raised his arms and separated them.

"And all of this is ours to use." Rico chuckled

It also had one large fresh water pool. All of the pools had a large water slide and a spring board. Three of the pools had three meter boards. "Pick your poison" as the boys would say. You had to go off every spring board and down every slide. Those were "the boys" rules. The pools also had a total of thirty swinging rings. What a place!

Sutro's provided a 2,700 seat amphitheater for shows, five hundred seventeen private dressing rooms, lockers to rent and public dressing rooms for everyone else. After spending several hours of  fun in the different pools, they would have one last adventure in Sutro's. It had San Francisco's only ice skating rink! None of the boys had ever skated before, so they spent much  of there time holding on to the side walls. They would  fall  a lot when they ventured away from those walls. Eventually, they got some what the hang of it. Making around the rink without falling was the goal. There butts and wrists were so sore when they were done, but they had so much fun laughing and pointing at each other falling. LeRoy even fell forward one time hitting his chin on the ice.

"Dam Tex. You alright/" Johnny and Rico knelt down on the ice to help LeRoy get up.

Laughing Tex said "Sure thing. How about you two?" As he yanked them to the ice.

Dan was laughing too. "That's one hell of a sight."

The three kids sat in a large lump on the ice laughing at each other.

By six that night, it was time to grab some dinner.  A couple more "Coney Island Red Hots" for a dime each seemed like a pretty good idea. They found some pretty cheap beef jerky at one of the concession stands that  they could snack on the rest of the night. The guys were getting tired but they still had several hours left. They would stay until they had just enough money for the ride home.

They made sure that they stayed away from any of the games, so they could get as many rides in as possible. There were times they would run to each ride, but at the end of the night, they were walking. As ten at night rolled around, they were down to the ten cents it would cost to get each home.

It seemed like a long walk up Ocean Boulevard, but they finally made it to the Market Street Express. Once on the electric car, three of the boys fell asleep. Danny was still excited about today's adventures. He figured he would sleep when he got home. The final ten minute ride on the 29 car got them back to Third and Evens. After getting off the car in front of DeNikes Cafe, they stood around laughing and talking about what went on that day. They were tired and there legs were sore from all of the walking and swimming.

"See you guys tomorrow around eleven." Johnny reminded the guys that they had a one o'clock baseball game at Visitation Valley. They'd catch the 18 car which would get them to the field in time for the game.. There wouldn't be any ice cream at Moody's and no movie this Sunday after the game. They were all out of money and Johnny and Rico had work on Monday morning. Dan and Tex would tell some great stories at school for the next week.

The next couple of weekends the boys would spend there time over at the at Bayview fields playing baseball or at the corral on Kirkland learning how to rope and ride. Many people, boys, girls and adults would show up on Sunday afternoons to watch and bet on the horse races. There was one rider who was really good. Her name was Nellie. She was only fifteen just like the boys. Nellie won most of her races even though the other riders were usually older men.. She went to All Hallows School like many other of the Catholic girls in the area. At All Hallows the girls had to wear a uniform.  After school she would hustle over to the corral and change into her riding cloths to ride her two horses and work out any other horse that needed it. Nellie wore blue genes with the pant legs rolled up three to four inches. Her cowboy boots were well used and a dirty brown. She always had a short sleeve button down shirt with the sleeves rolled up too. Her long blonde hair was covered with a bandanna. Each day it would be a different color. Being quiet, she wasn't to popular with kids her own age, especially the girls.

Nellie and Johnny became friends when they were a lot younger because of all the time they spent at the corral together. She would help him with his bulldogging and give him tips on how to ride better. Brew, one of her horses that Johnny rode a lot, was a tall Appaloosas . He had a white head and main with a black stripe covering his eyes and mouth. The rest of his body was black with four white socks below the ankles. Nellie's other horse was named Scampers. He was a smaller quarter horse she used for racing. Scampers was a brownish red horse. No other colors. When the sun hit him in the summer, he turned a beautiful bronze. Nellie liked to show Scampers off when she could. You would often see her riding around the neighborhood. and she always rode over to watch "the boys" playing baseball at Bayview fields. Johnny and Nellie would take Brew and Scampers up to Bayview Hill and ride in the large pastures. That was great for the horses and Johnny had a lot of fun chasing after the faster Nellie.

# CHAPTER FIVE
## BACK TO SCHOOL

Two years into the Great Depression, things were starting to get difficult for everyone, even in the Butchertown area.  With the railroad running along Third Street into the City, it brought many men of all ages and ethnic back rounds looking for work. Just like all big cities and small towns, there wasn't much work for the new comers. Those who had jobs when the stock market crashed in October 1929, were struggling to hold on to them. Many had lost them. New York had Hooverville for the out of work homeless people, San Francisco's version was in Hunters Point. People lived in larger cement pipes, built shelters out of old wood pallets, spare wood, card board and anything else that would block the wind and rain. By now all of the Chinese shrimp farms had disappeared from along the bay front. The Hoe bow's who lived in the shacks could often be seen harvesting what shrimp still lived in the shallows of the bay. Fishing for bottom fish also helped feed the unfortunate.

For Johnny and Rico, work had become on and off in the last two years. When they weren't working, they started back at school. They decided that if they were going to get anything done at school, they had to attend different schools. Rico started back at Commerce High School in Visitation Valley. Johnny began attending classes at Galileo, which was downtown off Van Ness Ave. Both High Schools were easy to get to by using the street cars that ran twenty four hours a day.

Rico got off to a better start at Commerce than Johnny did at Galileo. Almost all of the kids from the Butchertown area all went to Commerce. Rico knew many people there already, so being "the new guy" in classes was easy. He was a little behind academically but he managed. During that time Rico met Genny, a nice girl who lived off of Paul Avenue. They hit it off and began to date when Rico could manage to come up with a few bucks.

Johnny, on the other hand, knew no one at Galileo except Red Stevens. Turnbull and Red had gone to school together since the first grade. They were good buddies through out grade school. Red had been going to Galileo since his freshmen year full time. He had become part of the schools community. He worked hard to fit in with others. Red had also become a success on the football field and was one of the top players. Through Red, Johnny would eventually become friends with many of the athletes. Johnny dressed different than most of the other guys. The plaid long sleeve shirts and blue jeans rolled up four or five inches, was a dead give away of where he lived! He also sounded different when he talked. The Butchertown accent. Johnny didn't say much to people he didn't know. And minded his own business. Eventually he did become friends with many. There were one or two that thought he was easy to pick on that first year.

The tall thin kid from Butchertown first showed his ability to take care of himself while waiting for a street car after school one day in January 1930. A group of older boys that were dressed in very nice clothes, decided to make fun of the "hick" with cowboy boots and jeans.

"Hey Butchertown Boy, you can get on after we do." Hamilton Lawrence was a Senior and popular kid and one of the Student Body Officers.

Johnny, not wanting any trouble, decided to step back and let the four boys in front of him. When the street car arrived, the four got on but they made it so that the car took off without Johnny. They all pointed at Turnbull through the windows and laughed at him. Hamilton flipped Johnny the finger as he chuckled. Johnny had to wait for the next car.

The next day, after school, Johnny was again waiting for the street car when the same four boys approached.

"Well, well. It's Butchertown Johnny ! You can get to the end of the line." Hamilton smirked as the other three boys gathered around Johnny.

"Not today." Johnny said with a smile. " I'm first on."

"Maybe you don't understand! Your kind can wait." Hamilton wasn't smiling now.

"And what is my kind?" Johnny was sure where this was going, but he didn't know how the rich kids started fights. This wasn't the corral.

"Your not even second class. Your dirt!" Hamilton put his hand on Johnny's chest and pushed him backwards into one of the three boys standing there.

In Johnny's mind, that was as good as knocking a block of wood off his shoulder. He laughed, and rolled up the sleeves of his shirt. Hamilton took his coat off and handed it to a boy on his left.

"Kick his ass Hamilton." Cried another

Even though Hamilton was two years older and heavier than Johnny, it was no contest. Johnny had done this many times in the past.

Johnny's first punch landed just below Hamilton's right eye, the second came right behind it to the Seniors nose. As the blood trickled out, he took a step back.

"You just got lucky. I'm ready now." With his hands up higher, the older boy came at Turnbull.

Johnny took a step to his left and popped out a jab. Hamilton blocked this one with his left hand, leaving his chin wide open. Johnny didn't need to move his feet just his quick right fist. With the twist of his hips, the punch landed right on Hamilton's open mouthed jaw.

"Any one else?" Johnny looked at the three boys that were standing. He looked at Hamilton lying on the ground, with his eyes rolled up and said.

"I guess I'm getting on first tonight and every night."

Word got around at school the next day. Hamilton recruited a bigger and tougher Senior friend to "teach" Johnny Turnbull a lesson'. This altercation took place at lunch in the courtyard. It surprised Johnny when Hamilton and his friend approached him and tried to bully Johnny. Once things got started, it took "Butchertown John" longer to subdue the big guy than it did Hamilton. Turnbull had one advantage, he was very experienced at fighting and very good.. Two teachers who were walking through the courtyard noticed a big crowd in a circle and a lot of yelling. After working there way through the students, they pulled Johnny off of Hamilton's friend. They then picked up the bloody boy off of the grass and took both to the schools main office. They both missed the next three days of school, but that was the end of anyone picking a fight with the kid from Butchertown.

As the school year finished in June of 1932, Johnny had become very comfortable at school. He made many friends. He had gotten to know many of the boys on the soccer and basketball teams. The football players that Red introduced to Johnny during the year talked to him about trying to play football. He put a lot of thought into the idea. Rico and Johnny both wanted to play, but they had only played sandlot ball at the fields for fun. John talked it over with Ma and Rita about how it would affect the family.

It was decided that if there was no work, he should go to school and play. Rico and his parents felt the same way. It would be a good thing for the boys to be at school learning and working to graduate. Plus the experiences they were having were just what they needed. To be kids and have fun with others their own age. Work would start soon enough.

The summer of 32 for the two seventeen year old's, John Turnbull and Rico Landucci, was not very exciting. With not much money for fun things to do and only occasional work, Johnny, Rico, LeRoy and Danny spent much of their time over at the corral. Johnny was getting better at his bull dogging. His riding, thanks to Nellie, had improved over the year. This aloud him to concentrate more on his technique of turning the steer to the ground. He enjoyed wrestling the steers and all of the playful kidding around with the four friends. They also would spend the real hot days at the cove swimming and even got a few Sunday baseball games in.

As the second week of August came around, Johnny arrived at the Galileo gym on a Monday morning at 7:00. Joe was off to Commerce High Schools gym also. Johnny was early for the 9:00 practice. He had to check out his football gear and get his locker and lock. Red Stevens, meet him there, and helped him out getting his gear on right and showing him around a little. Johnny was really nervous. Having never played organized football, he didn't know what to expect. He was the only Senior trying out for the team that had never played before. Coach Ras Johnson was a thirty plus year old coach. He had a round head and face with very little yellow hair. His five foot eight inches held his 210 pounds very well. Coach had spent four years in the United States Marines at the end of the war. He went to the University of San Francisco after the war and played four years of football for the Dons. Coach Johnson had been teaching at Galileo since he graduated in 1926.

He always wore football pants and some kind of white tee shirt with a Lion on it. On top of his head, he had a crooked baseball cap with the block letter G, a whistle around his neck and the clip board, always a clip board, with plenty of paper filled with his notes and diagrammed plays.

In the locker room before the players went to the practice field, Coach Johnson had a short talk with Turnbull about his chances of ever playing. He was pretty blunt saying that John most likely would never suit up for a game. He also made it clear that if he didn't work hard at learning, or missed a practice, he would be cut from the team. Johnny was disappointed to hear what Coach told him, but appreciated his honesty. With his mind made up, he was going to give his best effort to be the best player he could become and be a good teammate.

Eighty five players checked out gear for the Galileo Lions football team. Being apart of that many players who knew what was going on and not knowing anything himself made things very difficult.

Walking out of the locker room, which was off of the gym and on the way to the practice field, Red Stevens and Nick Holoski grabbed Johnny.

"You nervous Rock?" Red asked

"I think so! Nervous and excited! But I don't know where to go or what to do." Johnny said as he struggled to put on the leather helmet.

"Just follow me today." Nick slapped Johns shoulder pads. " A couple of us lineman, we'll take care of ya. Coach can sometimes come off as an ass, but he is just looking for ways to test you. See what your made of. Like the Marine he is."

Running, exercising and doing some of the drills with gear and helmet on took some time to get used to. The leather helmet and chin strap pinched his forehead and ears. After five practices, his forehead skin was getting raw and his ears pink. He did find that as time went on, the sweat began to help mold the helmet to the shape of his head making it easier to wear. The cotton practice jersey and pants were just plain hot and itchy. It also took some time to adjust to the leather shoulder pads and the elastic straps that went under his arm pits to hold the pads in place. They began to rub his skin raw until he started to wear a tee shirt  under them. It was hot, but they didn't rub anymore.

To get some extra work in, Johnny would get to practice

early every day and stay after each night.  Bill Roberts, Buck Bailey, Sebastian Passanisi, Nick Holoski and Big Frank Stefani took turns "Coaching him up." The Coaches could not spend  any time with the new guy who couldn't do much.

The first thing Johnny had to learn was his stance. Putting his hand down on the ground and being balanced with all of the gear on took some time. Coaches would not allow him in any of the live drills until he learned how to get into and out of his stance. He watched a lot during the first few practices. He did all of the running and exercises, but no live contact against other players. He was allowed to hit dummies and he did a lot of work against the dummies before and after practices.

By Thursday, Coach Johnson told Johnny before practice that he needed to take some live repetitions and see if he still wanted to continue to play.

After the pre practice warm ups, Coach blew his whistle and called out some directions for the players to get to there practice stations. Things were really confusing, with guys running in all different directions, but Johnny followed Nick and the rest of the lineman for there fundamental work against some dummies.

Finally Coach Johnson called out.

"Lets get the dummies off to the side. Partner up and lets get some one on ones done. Turnbull, make sure you line up with Holoski."

Nick raised his eye brows and looked at Johnny.

"Come on Bud, lets line up over here."

The players would get into there stances and Coach would

yell the cadence out and the players would try to block each other. Holoski was an experienced player and one of the top lineman. He was big and strong. Johnny's heart began to race as he started to get himself ready for his first contact. What would it be like? Would it hurt? Hell, he'd been kicked by cows and run over by hogs. He'd wrestled steers. It couldn't be any worse. He thought, I even have all of these pads and a helmet on to protect myself!

It didn't take long before it was his turn!

"Holoski, you better not take it easy on Turnbull."

Both players got into their three point stance and looked into each others eyes. Holoski showed no fear. The sweat dripped off his nose and down the sides off his face on both sides. The sweat cleared away the dust on his face causing streaks. Johnny could hear Nick breathing and Johnny could see his nostrils opening and closing.

"On One! On One!" Called out Coach Johnson.

"Set"

Johnny clinched his teeth together as he sat in his stance. He was ready.

"HUT One"

Holoski exploded on the T of hut. Not waiting for the one. Experience told him that was a great way to get the jump on someone. From his stance, Nick took the six inch first step that he was taught. The step was straight at Johnny with his shoulders low and his eyes looking at his target. The target was just below Johnny's chin. Johnny moved too, but his movement was straight up! Not good for Turnbull. Holoski placed his face in Johnny's chest and ripped both forearms into Turnbulls body. With his feet running, he lifted Turnbull in the air and drove him into the dirt about five yards from the start. The back of Johnny's head was the first thing to hit the ground. When Holoski's forearms first hit Johnny, all of the air in his lungs blew out of his mouth. At least he kept his eyes open.. His body was numb ! After Nick got off of Johnny, he reached down to help him up to his feet.

"Good Job Holoski! Turnbull! You can't stand up like that! You gotta get low! Next." Coach Johnson moved to the next pair.

"Sorry Bud, but I had too."

Coughing, Johnny replied while shaking his head.

"I know. Thanks Nick for the ride." They both laughed.

The players rotated so they could go against some one different. They each got three live reps. Johnny's next two opponents were Passanissi and Bailey. Both were going to be starters for the team. Johnny didn't do very good against either player. As they moved to another station, Coach Johnson walked up to Johnny.

"Well Turnbull, I guess you've had enough. You can turn you gear in after practice."

"Are you cutting me from the team Coach?" Johnny asked

"No, I just figured after getting your butt kicked so bad, you'd want ta quit."

No way Coach! Those guys have put in extra time to help me out. I can't quit on them. I may not be very good, but I wont quit. No matter what happens!"

As Coached walked away, Johnny's head began to throb. His chest hurt. He found out with those three reps how physical football can be.

The rest of the two a day practices that week were much of the same. It became evident very quickly who the better players were. Coach Johnson was beginning to put together his teams. The first split of players took place on Friday morning when the freshmen and Sophomores began to do team work separately after fundamentals. Johnny stayed with the "Varsity." By the end of the week, everyone walked around with tan lines on there legs and arms. It was kinda funny to see the different lines of color on the bodies in the shower after practice. Johnny's skin had turned red on the lower part of his legs just above his calf. This is where the practice pants stopped. He also had a red "Farmers tan" on his arms. Some of the guys turned a dark brown.

Trying to learn not only how to play the game, but to learn the plays, was extremely difficult. The offense used its own language! It had a numbering system to go along with names for each position. Confusing. Nick and Red tried to help Johnny learn after each practice but it was going slow. The offense had words like: Buck Trap, Buck Sweep, Buck Option, Buck Sweep Pass, Power, Power Sweep, Reverse, Power Counter and numbers that went along with the words. The offense used what was called series football. The Buck Series and the Power Series. "Buck" told the lineman certain things as well as "Power". Then there was the defensive plays. The "Base" defense was a six man line with two linebackers. The lineman had to know how to :slant, along with playing in different gaps. The Linebackers had to be good at "reading" the offensive guards. They also used a"four two defense when the other team was going to pass the ball. The key to defense was to make sure that you at least lined up correctly.

At the start of the second week of doubles, Coach Johnson put together his first eleven and his second eleven. Football in the 1930's was a brutal game. Like baseball, when you came out of the game, you could not go back in. The only substitutions happened when someone got hurt or a team was so far ahead in the fourth quarter they might get some of the twos in. But that rarely happened. Players had to play offense, defense and all of the kicking game plays.

"You guys on the first team, need to get better or one of the twos will replace you. This is where we start. Things can change by next week. You number two's must push the ones to keep their spots."

He looked at the remaining players, which Johnny was part of. " We will only suit up the ones and twos for games. So, you can either quit or beat out a number two. It's up to you."

Johnny liked the coaches approach to things. Every thing was cut and dried. If you didn't like it, you could do something to change it. At the start of the second practice that day, a few of the number threes and fours were not there. Johnny's goal was to earn a spot with the two's so he could suit up.

Watching from the stands with 13,000 others at Kezar Stadium, Johnny saw the Lions beat Poly 7 to 6 in the first game of the season. Red kicked the winning extra point in the third quarter. On September 15th at Kezar, the Lions came from behind in the fourth quarter when Red tossed a touchdown pass to Phil Hull for a 6 to 2 win over Balboa. Coach Johnson had made several switches during the next week. True to his word, one of the number ones was moved to the twos and three twos got demoted to the threes. Johnny moved up to the number three squad. Johnny was getting better. He was playing end on both offense and defense. Coach had started to rotate him in with the twos during scrimmages.

"Turnbull, you need to learn your plays in the kicking game. If your ever going to suit, that will make a difference."

"Got it Coach  Johnson."

Game three took place in Stockton. Only the ones and several twos made the  five hour bus ride on September 30th.

The game ended in a 19-19 tie. Red tossed three touchdown passes! On the 12th of October in Kezar, Galileo shut out Lowell 7-0. Lowell was the Lions arch rival. It was a very physical game. The Orange  and Purple from Lowell lost three players to injuries that day. Just before halftime, Big Frank dislocated his little finger on his left hand. It was pointing sideways and Frank was in a lot of pain. Coach Johnson called a timeout and pulled Frank into a defensive huddle. He grabbed his hand and yanked the little finger back in place. The pain went away. At halftime Coach wrapped some tape around the finger and Frank played on.

On the 22ed of October, the Commerce Bulldogs came to Kezar. Johnny watched the game with his good friends Rico, LeRoy and Danny . Rico was in the same situation as Johnny. He wasn't a one or two, but he was getting close! He would make the twos the next week and the last week of the season Rico  made it as a one and played against Balboa. Galileo, behind a touchdown pass from Red and a five yard line buck by fullback George Lapin beat Commerce. The Lions remained undefeated with the 14-6 win. Going into the Sacred Heart game, injuries through the season were beginning to take their tole. Galileo was no exception. Johnny was also getting lots of nicks and bumps,but practice just wasn't as fierce as the games. Johnny was still getting close to getting a chance to suit up. It didn't happen this week. Galileo then beat Sacred Heart but the same score of 14-6, setting up a final game for the City Championship against Mission.

With this being the last week of the season, Johnny didn't really want it to end. Early in the season, he would sit in his last period class and dread going to practice. Nick Holoski, Frank Stefani and Sebastian Passanisi were really taking it to him. Knowing that you are going to get your fanny handed to you, isn't a pleasant feeling. But, he continued to show up. Nick, Frank, Sebastian and the other Seniors continued to encourage him. Even though he hadn't suited up, he felt part of the team. That was a good thing for him. By the fifth game week vs Lowell, Johnny made several plays in Tuesdays scrimmage. Playing on defense with the twos at defensive end, he tackled Red several times and smashed into Phil Hull knocking him out of practice. The next week during the scrimmage he again became noticed by Coach Johnson. Although Johnny could not beat Nick, Frank and Sebastian, he could now hold his own. He decided that the scrimmages would become "His Games".He loved to play football and only wished he had played the year before.

Before Mondays practice, Coach Johnson called Johnny into his office. Twirling his whistle on his finger.

"Turnbull! You have really come on these last couple of weeks. I figured you would have quit by now. But you are giving our offensive ends all they can handle. I feel you have become our third best end on defense."

Sitting behind his deck, he put his whistle around his neck and placed his cap on his head and stood up.

"That being said, your still not there yet on offense and I'm not sure about the kicking game. So, this Friday I'm not going to have you dress for the game against Mission. But ... I want you on the sideline with your teammates. You deserve that much."

Not sure how to feel or what he should say, Johnny gave it

some quick thought. After the pause.

"Ah Coach" Followed by another pause. "Thank you for always being straight up about everything. I believe what you're saying. It would be really something to be able to suit up Friday, but we need to win this game. It will be an honor to be with the guys on the sideline during the game. I'll still go hard this week to try to change your mind and help us get ready. Thanks Coach".

"Johnny, you've improved so much this season. More than any other player. You're the hardest working player that we have. At the beginning of daily doubles, I didn't think you would stick it out. I tried to make you quit. But you didn't and I'm glad you came out."

Johnny left the coaches office at a quick pace and hustled out to practice. He had four practices left of football and he was going to make the best of them. By this time of the season, Johnny had become used to the hitting. The soreness either had gone away, or he just didn't feel it. He was amazed how the body could adapt to such punishment. He also discovered how important the mind was in playing football. It controlled the pain but also was very important in knowing what to do before it happened. Also, being able to react in split seconds based on what you saw and what you felt was also very important.

In Front of 15,000 fans at Kezar Stadium in Golden Gate Park, the Mission Bears scored twice by pass in the second quarter to take a 13-0 lead. The rest of the game was played between the twenty yard lines as neither team could manage much of a drive to threaten the goaline. As the clock ticked down, Johnny could feel the disappointment of his teammates, coaches and with in himself. It would have been great to be a champion. It just wasn't meant to be.

After the game in the quiet locker room, players showered

the mud and grime off of them then sat around and talked with each other. Johnny was going to get a ride back to Butchertown with Red, but first the Seniors were going to a restaurant for dinner. Nick, Frank, Phil, along with the other Seniors made sure Red brought Johnny along. For Johnny, it was a great feeling to be thought of like that by his friends who considered him a teammate.

The next two weeks at school were anything but exciting. Johnny really missed going to practice, the camaraderie with the players that had developed and because there wasn't any kind of punishment for missing a day of school, he began to miss classes. He would instead, check into he Teamsters Union Hall before school each day. It was close to the high school. If there was a Union job, Johnny would take it instead of going to school. When the semester ended, he decided to visit with a school counselor to see how close he was to graduating. No matter what he did, he would not have enough credits to graduate. He would have to go to night school to complete his education.

After church during the Christmas break from school, Johnny ran into Jack Allen. Things had been picking up in the meat business and Allen's was going to need a full time driver for a route across the bay on the ferry.

"Say Johnny, how are you doing these days?"

"Just going to school and getting some work out of the Union Hall." Johnny shook hands with Mr. Allen.

"I'm going to need a route driver really soon. Oakland and parts of the East Bay. You ready to come back to work?"

"Mr. Allen ... You say the word and I'll be there."

Two weeks later, Johnny got a call from Big John Bishop. Big

John, the Marine Veteran from World War I, was also the head mechanic for Allens Truck garage.. He also managed the drivers.

"Johnny! This is John Bishop! I need a driver. Mr. Allen told me to give you the first call. You want a full time job with us?"

"When do I start?" John was excited to get back to work. High school had been something different and football was worth doing. He made some good friends but it was time to get back to work and start his adult life.

And so the next day Johnny restarted his life at Allen's. It would last the rest of his life.

# CHAPTER SIX
## THE STRIKE

As time rolled on, Johnny began to settle into his job driving. His delivery route was in the East Bay. Every morning he would have to load his truck with the orders from the loading dock. His route sheet was written down in the order of each delivery. Because his truck didn't have refrigeration, he had to hustle loading everything and get off of the dock. He was glad that everything had already been weighed and written down. There were four loading docks. The East Bay route had to be the first group of trucks loaded because of the distance it had to travel. Plus it had to catch the first Ferry to cross the Bay to Oakland. The Golden Gate Bridge had just begun its construction. It would not be completed until 1937. The Bay Bridge had also begun its construction to connect San Francisco to Oakland and the East Bay. It would be finished in early 1936.

Rico was back working at Allens in the Pork Room. The Pork room was really a large part of the complete lower floor of the newly built complex that took up Evens Avenue all the way to Mendell. This floor prepped the slab bellies for bacon,separated the ribs and all other cuts from the hogs. The stomach linings and intestines were placed in ice filled gondolas and moved by elevator upstairs on the second floor along with the hams. The gondolas filled with the stomach and intestines were usually sold to the Chinese butcher shops or bought by the Chinese restaurants. The hams were smoked in the second floor smokehouse. LeRoy McDavid had just graduated from Commerce High School in June and was working the kill floor at Moffatt's, which was across the street on Evens Ave from Allens. It wasn't as big as the Allens kill floor. At Allens it was on the second floor of the building. At Moffats, it was on the street floor. LeRoy had several jobs which he performed. Usually rotating those jobs with other workers. The "Kill" floors were set up  like assembly lines only in reverse order!. They were messy and loud. The area where the beef and lambs were processed was separate from the hog killing area. The beef were killed first, followed by the lambs and then the hogs last. As soon as the lambs were done, the clean up crew began washing down the whole area. Next to the killing areas where the coolers that housed the sides and quartered beef which were pushed around on rails hanging from the ceilings. Before the beef were placed in the coolers, they were wrapped with wet cloth shrouds. When they were pulled off the next day, the fat was smooth and looked better to those who would buy the beef. The lams were hung also on the second floor coolers. The hogs were quit a process. The hair on the skin of the hogs had to be shaved off by using rocks of rosin. This was usually done by the new guys. It was a very difficult job. Years later they would drag the hogs thru boiling water to burn off the hair.

Danny Cary was doing a summer job moving cows,hogs and

sheep around in the Allen's corrals on Newhall. He had to make sure they were ready for the kill floor. Moving the hogs to the killing area was the most difficult. It was like they could smell what was coming. He often had to use baseball bats to the head of the hogs or tie a rope noose around the head and drag them. The large sows were really difficult and mean. The sheep were the easiest. He used four or five "Judas" sheep. They knew the way to the area and the others just followed them. He would use those sheep all summer. The beef just needed a swat on the butt to get them where they needed to go. Danny would start his Senior year at Galileo High School in the fall. Everyone was glad that they had jobs, but the work was long and difficult. It was cold in the winter months, and very hot in the summer.

Work around San Francisco had picked up by 1934. The Port of San Francisco was the busiest port along the entire West Coast. It also employed twenty five percent of the work force in San Francisco. The working conditions up and down the coast along the docks and piers for longshoreman and the warehouse workers had always been horrendous at best. The hiring process along the piers had also always been corrupt. The shipping industry since the 1850's, especially in San Francisco, controlled the politicians and the local police. Many of those politicians and police received kick backs from the Industrial Association, which represented the shipping companies. They bought the politicians off to control laws and make policies that made operations easier and more profitable. The police were there to provide protection, allowing the shippers to control the work force.

Some of Johnny's friends from the Galileo Football team were working as longshoreman. Nick Holoski, Frank Stefani and Art "Pete" Peterson had started work at the docks after high school. There were several others who worked in the warehouses on the piers. Also working at Allens, on the kill floor, was Red Stevens. Red's nick name was "Easy Money" because he was always bitching at how hard the work was. Later on he would always call the new guys "Easy Money" as a joke. Red was like many of the "line" workers. He did many jobs on all three butchering lines. Most of the guys were very good with a knife. Carl Schott also worked on the kill floor. Carl was perched high above the floor. He tied off the rear end of the beef as they passed by him. Guys just called him by his nick name.."Moon".

Johnny would run into those guys at O'Doul's Bar. Although still under the legal drinking age, no one ever checked them. The young men also enjoyed the Anchor Steam Beer that The Dog Patch Saloon served. They also enjoyed talking about working conditions at the docks as well as in Butchertown.

Wearing a brown cowhide vest over a wool long sleeve shirt rolled up to the elbows, Nick started things off on this Friday night after spending a ten hour shift on the docks.

"If we get picked in "The Shape Up", we work our ass off ten hours for nine stinking bucks. Two bits goes to the picker."

He then grabbed his beer mug, took a gulp and slammed it to the table. Nick was fired up!

"The Shape Up" is the process of hiring workers for the different jobs. Longshoreman gather in crowds in front of the Picker each morning. He decides who works where and when. He'll call out the pier number and point at the workers. One by one they head off and start work. Not everyone gets chosen. At the end of each shift, the workers pay off the Picker. The usual fee is two bits (twenty five cents). Some times guys will pay more, some less, but you better pay! These guys were also members of the International Longshoreman's and Warehousemans Union ( ILWU).

Frank was sitting in between Johnny and Red. His cap was always worn backwards on a rather large head.  The growth on his face was only a days worth, but thick. Frank liked to sit with his chair backwards so that he could rest his arms or elbows on the back. As was the working mans style of dress, he too  wore a plaid shirt with a long John shirt underneath it.

"Yesterday I  spent ten hours in the hold of a dark cargo ship. It was freezing, damp and stunk of some kind a shit! I know you Butchertown guys are used to that!" They all laughed.

"But come on, Rats? Big some bitches! And a lot of them. No place to sit for a break, no place to set a lunch pale. Later in the day, it becomes a hot box. My shirt was soaked. Plus there is no where to piss or shit! For less than a buck an hour." The look on his face was of disappointment and anger.

"Pete" then chipped in.

"No kidding. It sucks everyday. The rain and damp fog on deck! Work doesn't stop because your wet. Guys in prison have a better life. Think about That! Things have to change."

Rico asked Nick. " You guys are part of a union right? Don't they help?"

Nick laughed. "Hell! They were getting kick backs too. But things have changed. We got a new guy who worked on the docks. He gets it! He understands things. Harry Bridges is his name. He wants to make changes. He has been working on it!'

A young upstart had risen in the ranks of the union, who would not be bought off. Harry Bridges had become the first President of the ILWU. Harry had come to San Francisco in 1920 from Australia to work on the docks. He was a member of the "Star Gang". They had a reputation of the hardest,toughest and best group of longshoreman, not only in San Francisco, but along the

West Coast. Though of slight build, Harry's hands were large and calloused. When he shook someones hand, it was like a vise. Harry sported a lot of curly black hair. It looked much like Rico's hair, but Rico was starting to lose his! When talking with the working class guy, he dressed just like them. It was comfortable, but also put the guys in a good place. He was, after all, one of them. Even though he talked funny, with the usual Australian twist and vocabulary, he was well understood. They liked his message and ideas. He had spent time on the docks "taking care of business" so to speak with guys who didn't like some of his ideas of really unionizing the workers.

Using his reputation and being a smart and charismatic man, Harry had acquired the backing of the longshoreman and those working in the warehouses. The shipping companies, Northwest Shipping of America, Eclipse Shipping Inc. and Del Monte Canning, were looking for ways to get him out of power. Nothing seemed to work. Harry was also enlisting the help of other local unions and trying to organize a brotherhood among all workers. Harry was usually seen talking with small groups of all workers in the local drinking establishments around town. Harry liked his beer and would never pass up a good strong High Ball. His personalized conversations with many young, as well as older workers, helped him gain even more support and confidence in his quest to get better working conditions for all labor workers.

Johnny had spent several hours with Harry the last week of February at DeNikes Tavern. Red Stevens, LeRoy McDavid, Rico Landucci and several of the other young butchers and teamsters from the Butchertown area also visited with Harry and his lawyer Robert Silver. Johnny was very interested in what Harry and Robert were trying to accomplish. Working conditions in Butchertown were better than those on the docks because of the specialized skills, but not by much. The long hours for very little pay hadn't changed in the business. You were not going to get rich by working in Butchertown. The workers for the different slaughter houses did get the opportunity to buy there meat at wholesale prices. That helped in the pocket books, but not much. Workers also did not have medical or dental benefits. Guys very seldom went to a doctor and never to a hospital. If workers got injured at work or became sick, they went without pay for as long as they stayed at home. Because there were so many men looking for work, the large companies had great leverage when it came to paying workers. Harry Bridges and his newly appointed union leaders were working very hard to change that.

"What do you think about all of this Frank?"
Rico was leaning to the side of the unions idea of going on strike.

"I listen to my father a lot. He's been working on those docks and piers since the quake. Things haven't changed since he started there. He thinks that we should take advantage of a guy like Harry. He likes the idea of going on strike!

Frank took a long pull off of his mug. He then took his sleeve across his mouth and said.

"I'm in. I don't want to do what my old man has done for the rest of my life. I don't mind working hard, but I'd like to get paid for it. I don't like seeing those guys wearing suits and ties get all of the money."

That was the feeling of most of the labor workers around The City. The idea of striking was gaining momentum among the longshoreman. Harry Bridges and Silver were working hard with the other unions to gain there support because they knew that if they wanted things to change, it would take the whole City to do it.

Harry  and his lawyer, Silver, began meeting with the Industrial Association and its head negotiator, Hamilton Lawrence

Sr. The first week of February, Silver presented to Hamilton

"We'd like the workers to get paid a dollar ten cents an hour for a six hour work day and a thirty hour work week. We also want the union to set up who works and what shifts they work. No more "Shape Up."

"What? Why?" replied Hamilton

"This would allow more workers consistent work. The shorter hours per day per week, would cut down the amount of injuries on the job and keep workers healthy and working."

"Not going to happen!" He looked at Harry.

Hamilton Lawrence Sr. was dressed immaculately in a three piece brown double breasted pinned striped suit and a silk tie. At fifty five years old, he had been employed by the Association as its lawyer for twenty years. He had his hand in the connections with the last two Mayors and the City Council. He was also a drinking buddy with the Police Chief and the Police Commissioner.

"Your asking for way too much. Six hour work days and a thirty hour work week is not enough"

"Mr. Lawrence! This is just where we start. The future will eventually include; medical and dental benefits and paid leave. All of the things that you are privileged to." continued Silver. Robert had recently graduated from a small law school in Salem Oregon called Willamette University. Rob had spent some time working the docks in Seattle with Harry before going to school. The two had formed a strong friendship and shared the same values. He wasn't dressed as well as Hamilton but he was well spoken and very smart. His height of 6 foot 3 inches and athletic build gave him a strong presence.

Laughing Hamilton replied "Your crazy! The pathetic men that work the docks and in the warehouses are a dime a dozen. For every guy working, there are three waiting to work."

"Our guys are willing to strike. Walk out. Not only here in San Francisco, but Seattle, Los Angeles and the rest of the West Coast. We'll shut things down! You'll lose a lot of money Hamilton." Harry was not happy as he stood up and looked into Hamilton's eyes.

Hamilton stood up from behind his desk, put his cigar in its ash trey.

"It's against the law! The Police won't allow it. We have the press on our side and those who are not part of your union will not support the strike. We will hire enough strike breakers to get the work done. You can come back when you are ready to talk some sense."

Hamilton Lawrence knew that Harry was serious. He began plans for a strike. He talked with the Mayor and the Police Chief and Commissioner to prepare themselves for what was coming. He also had individual meetings with the newspapers editors and owners from up and down the Coast. They began writing editorials and articles that criticized the union and what a negative effect a strike would have on every one. They also began personalized attacks on Harry Bridges calling him a member of the Communist Party.

Each Monday Harry and Silver would approach Lawrence with the same demands. Each Monday would always end the same as the first meeting. The first Monday of April, Harry suggested that the shipping companies should also meet with Hamilton, Harry and his union board to begin working on a contract. The next three meetings didn't prove productive. Harry sensed this was just a ploy to drag things out. The union board , Harry and Silver spent those weeks of April talking with union members about striking. They were all behind the idea. On May first, Harry told the Industrial Association and the shipping companies, that they had until May eighth to start getting a contract done. With no agreement in site The International Longshoreman and Warehousemans Union workers of the West Coast declared a strike beginning May ninth.

The Association was prepared for the strike. They had organized strike breakers in each city. They housed these guys in compounds or on vacant moored ships in the areas. Police in each city would escort these workers to and from these ships and compounds to work each day. They also began to hire "out of work" criminals and armed them with axes, clubs and sometimes hand guns to intimidate the pickets.

On May fifteenth in the Port of San Pedro, just North of Oakland, strikers in San Pedro organized an attack on the compound of workers. During the attack, Police fired on the strikers, killing one and injuring many. Harry was not happy with the strikers. He didn't plan the attack. It made the union look bad, as newspapers up and down the coast continued to write damaging stories about the union and its leaders. People who were not striking, were siding with the Association. Every one now knew that this was going to take a great effort by the union and its men. They would need to be better organized and they would.

All of the young workers of the ILWU began to prepare for what they knew was coming. It was going to be long and difficult situation. They had been through a tough time with the depression, so they did have some experience with tough times. Knowing that they had a say in there future was exciting in a way. After the May fifteenth incident, twenty one of the other local and national unions began to see the importance of the strike. Teamsters, Seaman, Butchers and ship builders unions hoped to achieve higher wages, shorter hours and union control of hiring halls. On the first on July, 150,000 workers total from the twenty plus unions had joined in on the strike in San Francisco. Nothing was moving in or out of The City. It was completely shut down.

The first three days of July along with the fourth, were very quiet. The union had planned a demonstration for the fifth and the Association planned to "Open " things up on the same day. A perfect storm. The union fortified the pickets at the Ferry Building and along the piers of San Francisco. It continued to close down the three Ferries that carried travelers to and from Oakland and the rest of the East Bay. Around the City, all businesses came to a halt. Teamsters were not driving. Warehouses closed. Trains and public transportation had stopped.

The Association, having decided that this was the day to open the Port and the City, coordinated all of there resources and had them available. The hired toughs from out of town brought there ax handles, clubs and fists and they were backed by the San Francisco Police. In what the San Francisco Examiner and the Call-Bulletin would call "Bloody Thursday" in front of the Ferry Building, the strikers meet up with the strike breakers and the police.

The strikers were not intimidated. They too had ax handles clubs and fists. They would not back down and found safety in great numbers and a great cause.

"You know if we get up front of the line, we'll see who's coming for us and when."

Johnny looked at Frank, Nick and Rico, Pete was turned away checking things out. Tex and Danny hadn't got there yet, but were on there way. Red too, would also make it. Just off to the right were Mike Bishop and Sean Hannon, Johnny's old baseball teammates.

"Yo Bish"! Johnny yelled to Mike. Sporting a leather

cap,rolled up jeans, work boots and a fine mustache. Bish lifted his bat then took a puff of his cigar.

"Kick en some ass today Johnny !"

Hannon, who usually smiles a lot, was all business. The now filled out six footer was wearing his plaid work shirt rolled up to his elbow's. Led pipe in one hand and a set of brass knuckles in the other. With a bulging right cheek full of chew

"Butchertown Boys are ready!"

Harry Bridges was right up front about ten steps from the six young men. Right next to him was his trusted lawyer, Sliver. If his union workers were going to put themselves in danger over his ideas, he was going to be right next to them. He was sure that old Hamilton Lawrence Sr. was sitting in his office in his leather stuffed chair, smoking a cigar and drinking some fine Kentucky bourbon. Along side him was his twenty one year old son, who was a law student at the University of San Francisco.

" Your right. I don't like getting blindsided."

Frank had his cap on backwards and both sleeves rolled up. All four of the nineteen year olds were wearing Levi blue jeans that were rolled up a good five inches. They all wore thick soled black work boots. Johnny had a smoke dangling from the corner of his mouth. When he talked it bounced up and down. Nick had a long ax handle in his left hand with his right hand balled into a fist. His lower cheek was puffed out because of the chewing tobacco he was enjoying. Pete carried a smaller wooden handle but wore some brass knuckles over his right fist. Pete wasn't as big as Frank and Nick, more like Johnny, but not as tall. Pete was a  quick and fast guy that could give as good as he could take. Never afraid! Rico carried his old 28 oz baseball bat.

"I won't pop a cop until they touch me. But those pricks who work for the Association can kiss my Irish ass!"

"Pete! Your not Irish!" Johnny laughed.

"I know, but it sounded good!" They all smiled.

Red, Tex and Danny arrived together just at ten in the morning. Each carrying a baseball bat.

"Tex! What are you going to do with that? You never hit any thing with that before!" Rico started to giggle and the others broke out laughing. Tex was not a ball player.

"Hell. Those guys don't know I can't hit. But God Dam it, I'm here."

At a little after ten, the Police showed up in force and met up with the fifty or so armed thugs that were hired by the Association. They were there to escort the strike breakers past the demonstrators  to the docks and push back the large group of demonstrators from the Ferry.

"Scum!

Scabs!

Go Home!'

Came calls from the union workers to the strike breakers, police and thugs. Finally the mounted police showed up and it was obvious that they would lead the charge.

Harry and Silver approached the Police officer who seemed

to be in charge. They talked for what seemed forever, which was less that a minute.

As Harry and Silver walked back to the group of strikers, Harry called out

"Lets get ready men"!

"Don't get caught under those horses. Get to there side and grab there halters!" Johnny yelled to Nick, Frank and Pete. They hadn't been around horses before and got wide eyed when they saw them.

You'll be fine. Just stay calm"

BANG ! BANG! BANG! The police began to fire shots of tear gas into the crowd.

Harry yelled out "Stay tight men. Get close. Here they come."

The mounted police then rode into the crowd  followed by the foot patrol and the thugs. The eight young men cleared the mounted horses and went after the thugs. It became chaotic and nosy. Pushing, grabbing, punching and yelling among all participants took place. It was ugly. The police were forced back by the strikers several times but eventually the strikers were split up and began to retreat back a few blocks. Picket signs and trash littered the streets. People were in small groups and spread out.

Things had settled down for several hours while both sides took care of there injured and hurt. Johnny and his friends came out of the mess all intact. Frank had lost his cap! He also had to put his little finger back in place as it became damaged during the fracas.

"old football injury" Franks held up his finger before yanking on it. Everyone laughed.

Pete had blood on his brass knuckles. Johnny and Rico rolled up a couple of cigarettes and Nick put in a new chew.

"Dam! That was wild! You guys all ok  ?" Johnny made sure LeRoy and Danny were fine.

He put his hand on there shoulders and looked into there eyes.

"little different than a football game! Turnbull! Glad you're on our side. You throw some pretty good hands. You got a little pissed off."

Nick spit some chew juice on the street and punched Johnny lightly on his shoulder. And gave him a wink.

Everyone felt good about what they had done during the fight. They really liked what they saw from Harry and Silver! They saw Harry pull a thug down to the ground and repeatedly punched him in the face. They also saw Harry catch a few punches on the chin and kept fighting. Silver also gave a good showing. He was seen grabbing and  punching several thugs. With torn shirts, they walked through the strikers and made sure everyone was alright.

Looking up to the peaceful deep blue sky and sitting on the street curb, Johnny, Rico, LeRoy and Danny could see that the seagulls began to return to the area. They could hear them and there unique sound. The noise and commotion had scared them off. The pigeons were also returning to perch on the overhead electrical lines. Beyond the Ferry Building the Bays water was that same peaceful blue. Thin white caps formed from the slight winds blowing the fresh salty sea air to cool off the hot pavement and the hot tempers. The peace would not last long.

After getting some lunch provided by the union, several

strikers surrounded a police car that had driven up. Not wanting to let the officers out of the car, they began to shake it. That set things in motion again. This time the police, thugs and horseback riders came at full speed and not letting the strikers a chance to organize. Everyone sprinted to the area. More tear gas was fired into the crowds as the strike breakers tried to rescue those in the police car. Strikers began to throw rocks, empty cans, full cans and any thing else they could grab.. Face to face and hand to hand  fighting broke out. Being frustrated over the whole situation, several police from a short distance away fired rounds of shot gun shells into the strikers. . This caused the strikers to flee. They didn't have an answer for the shotguns.

With in the crowd of demonstrators were reporters from both The Examiner and The Call- Bulletin newspapers.  Those reporters saw and felt the terror first hand. They too ran from the police and thugs who now were beating on the fleeing demonstrators. They were trying to find places to take cover from the continuous shots. Men were falling from the shots. Others hobbled along. Many were helping each other find some where to hide.

Watching all of this happen from Rincon Hill, which was five blocks South, were hundreds of shocked  interested towns people. It looked like a Hollywood War movie, but it was real. Real men getting shot by there own police force. Again the birds fled and the noise became deafening.. The smoke and smell of the tear gas mixed with the powder and noise from the shot guns filled the area with despair.

Finally, what seemed like an eternity but was only minutes, the police came to there senses and stopped chasing and shooting. Luckily, only two of the union strikers were killed. Many, many were wounded and injured. Dozens went to the hospital. Many took care of themselves at there homes. Johnny had stayed close to Rico during the carnage but lost Tex and Danny. Sitting behind an old truck parked along the side of the road, they found both Danny and LeRoy. They still carried their bats in one hand but Danny was sitting holding his lower leg. Several bee bees from the shot gun had hit him during the run. . Eventually they wrapped a tee shirt around the wound to stop it from bleeding. Danny would later have his father take the bee bees out of his leg later when he got home. After a little more searching, they found Nick, Frank and Red. They all looked worse for wear. Bloody noses, torn shirts and dirty faces were common among them. Johnny and Rico rolled a cigarette and Nick gave Frank a chew and placed a rather large chew in his own upper lip to go along with the one in his lower lip.

With the cigarette bouncing, Johnny looked at everyone and said. "Any one see Bishop and Hannon?"

Tex looked at Johnny " I saw Bish on top of some Association guy , beaten his face in.! "

Danny was laughing " Hannon had two of those ass holes pinned in a corner with that pipe." Johnny cracked a big smile. " I knew those guys would be fine"

"Lets head over to DeNikes Tavern. Cyril will take care of us and we can get off our feet.'

"Sounds good. How far is it? Nick wasn't into long walks.

"Ah not far. It's on Third Street. Right near Allens". Red said quietly.

The walk back to DeNikes and Third Street took them past many of the on lookers from what the newspapers would call "Bloody Thursday". It was a good way to calm down and try to figure out what just had happened. Many of those on lookers could see in the eyes of these guys the effect it took on them. Some asked questions, but the young men were not in the mood to answer questions that they had almost no answers too.

Once at the Tavern, Cyril welcomed them and set them up at a large table in the back corner of the Tavern area. Being before five, the usual Thursday crowd of local workers began to make there way in. Some had been down at the demonstration, some had been on the Hill watching. It was definitely the talk of the town and inside the dimly lite tavern.

"I think we made a statement today! And I know the cops and the Ass - o- ciation also made one."

Johnny threw down his shot of bourbon that Cyril bought for each of the young men. Rico also washed out Danny's wound with some cheep whiskey.

"According to the Examiner, which just hit the streets, Your strike is gaining support from the people and the paper."

Cyril held up the front page showing the big headlines "Bloody Thursday!"

Bishop and Hannon rolled in at the same time and joined the boys at the long table.

"Cocktails" Hannon yelled as he went to the bar.

Bishop followed up with" Scotch Rocks!"

"Bloody Thursday" for the young men became Bloody Friday the next morning. Knowing that they would not have any work on Friday, they continued to toss down shots of bourbon and recap the day.

Johnny's final statement to his friends before they left was a slurred

"Sometimes you gotta do what ya gotta do, so that you can do what you want to do."

What he was saying was that he really didn't want to go through what that day had provided, but he had to so that they all could go forward and have better work conditions.

Nick and Frank followed Red to his house on Kirkwood. Pete went along with Rico to his place to sleep on the couch. Johnny was the last to leave. He and Cyril drank and talked for a short time. Leaving DeNikes, Johnny staggered and stumbled to home on Galvez a block away. He grabbed a coat and wool blanket from the downstairs closet and worked his way to the back porch. It would provide more protection from the early morning sun than the front porch. Johnny knew he would not make it up the stairs to his bed. He had done this before!

It was a rough night and morning. It didn't take long for the sky to start spinning. At first it was a slow spin and then it began to speed up. Getting to his feet, Johnny bent over the back railing and what was left in his stomach, came up. It helped stop the world from spinning long enough for him to curl up under the blanket with his head on the coat and fall asleep. The next morning he awoke to the smell of fresh coffee,frying bacon and a dry and horrible taste in his mouth. Unfortunately, the great smells accompanied a pounding headache. In fact everything hurt. He took some punishment during all of the exchanges on Thursday and now he was feeling the pain. He would drink a lot of that black coffee that morning, but only time, ,fresh air and sleep would cure his problems. He did chuckle knowing that everyone else felt the same.

The story that accompanied the headlines from the day before described the demonstration. It definitely told the strikers view as well as vividly describing the terror and blood shed of the second half of the day. It listed the two names of those killed and told stories of fleeing bodies. The descriptions and the stories of the day made it to every city's newspapers along the West Coast and even back East. The tied had turned for the union and its strikers. People began to really listen to Harry Bridges and the ILWU. The Examiner and The Call- Bulletin both printed  positive interviews with Harry along with powerful editorials against the police and the Association.

The fall out from the demonstration and newspapers accounts of it followed. The Governor called in the National Guard that night to stop the violence. The police no longer were in control. Both sides took steps back and Hamilton Lawrence Sr. gave Harry Bridges a call. They met each day for the next week to hammer out a contract.

On July 12th, 15,000 men from the twenty some local unions marched down Market Street in San Francisco. In what the Examiner called " A reverent procession", the men dressed in white shirts, white pants and white hats, walked the two miles to remind people of the two men that were killed and the many wounded on the fifth of July. All of the boys from Butchertown along with their new friends from the docks joined Harry , Silver and the other union leaders as they made a peaceful march down Market Street. After the march the boys got together at O'Doul's for some more beer and laughs and a toast to the two who had died.

The bonds that developed between the men would always be strong. The knew they had each others backs when needed.

Both sides  of the strike felt that the new contract favored them. What it did do for the union was open the door for future strikes and negotiations. The future would eventually bring the union workers more and more benefits. But the first contract got them a dollar an hour, nine hour work days that included breaks of up to an hour and union control of the hiring. No more "Shape Up"

For the young men who joined the fight on that Bloody Thursday, they became more involved in union business. Nick and Frank were recruited by Harry to help organize hiring processes on the docks. As the years went on they both became members of the union's board of directors. Johnny also stepped forward by representing the teamsters in the Butchertown Local. "Bloody Thursday" had profound effects on all of those who participated.

The Butchers Union lead by Robert Silver negotiated a new contract with the local slaughter houses. Pay was raised to $1.10 an hour. They also received a nine hour work day with a half hour break for lunch and two other fifteen minute breaks. They got paid for the eight hours of work. Forty hour work weeks became the normal. Any work over that would be considered "over time" and they would receive time and a half.

Silver also negotiated The Teamsters a salary based contract. They also received hiring control at the union hall and drivers would only drive five days in a row. Any thing after that and they would receive "over time " benefits.

Life did get back to somewhat normal. Johnny, Rico, LeRoy and Danny went to the big Rodeo in Salinas at the end of July. It convinced Johnny that next summer he would begin entering events. They also made a trip down to the Santa Cruz Boardwalk for more fun at the end of August.

# CHAPTER SEVEN
## TIME TO GO FISHING

The Boy's were always looking for things to do that would take them out of town. Any adventure that sounded like fun definitely wasn't off limits. They had spent many weekend days off of Candlestick Point hunting ducks and that was always fun. They had also fished in the bay and in the near by creek as kids but never had they fished in a lake or river.

"Johnny, Tex and you too Danny. What do you guys think about an over night'er by a lake fishing for some good ole trout?"

Rico had just arrived at Cyril's. Johnny and the boys were sitting at their normal spots at the end of the bar facing the front door.

"What are you talking about Rico?' Tex lifted his empty beer glass up at the bar tender and pointed at it as if to say another one. Danny and Johnny turned to face Rico. Both with puzzled looks.

"I was just thinking about something different to do for a change!" "Schmidt and Gilbert over in the Pork room were talking about them fishing at Lake Merced last weekend. They caught their share of trout. Couple of 20 plus inchers!"

"Just thought it sounded like it could be some fun."

"There is a place South of here in San Mateo County called Horseshoe Lake." Tex chipped in.

I heard that it's got it's share of luncker's!"

The boys sat for several hours talking about the advantages and disadvantages of that being a possibility for an adventure. Cyril also got involved in the conversation along with Hannon, Ross an Bishop. Sitting now around a large table they worked out the details of "Going Fishing".

Somebody needed to finalize things, so Johnny did.

"Alright then! We are going! Date is set for the fourth of July weekend. It's on a Tuesday this year!"

"So that means we leave Sunday morning sometime." Rico chipped in.

"How about after lunch, we drive down together. Leave from here." Hannon always liked to help organize things.

"Tex, that gives you a chance to eat lunch before we go."

"I'll pas. The way johnny drives, i'll get car sick."

On the second of July 1939, they all met at DeNikes parking lot at 11:00 am. Cyril was there also. They loaded up a fifteen and a half gallon beer keg out of the tavern's cooler that came along with a gravity flow tap. Cyril sold it to them for the same price he got from the Hamms Brewery. He also sold the boys eight half gallon jugs of cheap whiskey and four half gallon jugs of cheap tequila. The boys figured that what ever they didn't drink fishing, they could bring back and eventually get to it. They just didn't want to come up short.

"You got the meat Johnny?" Bishop asked.

"Yep. Eight large Hangers for Sunday night along with ten pounds of burger meat and a bunch of sausage dogs! Sal Barretta's special recipe." Sal worked in the Allen's sausage kitchen. E was in charge of mixing the different types of sausages they produced.

"Great! I got the potatoes, butter ect. Also, some Mac salad for all  f us and plenty of bread."

"Wilhelm, you got plenty of beans?"

"Yes sir . Of course. Only the best Butchertown Chili!"

They also brought a couple of axes a wedge, a splinting maul and a hand saw. They didn't want to be without wood for the camp fire.

Ross was in charge of the coffee. Fresh beans and pt. He also brought three grills to go over the fire to cook on. Tex took care of loading all of the cooking pans, knives, forks, spoons and the bacon and eggs for the mornings. Rico and Hannon loaded the beer keg up into a trailer that Hannon pulled behind his car. The keg sat in a special cooler with ice around it to keep it cold.

"Don't you guys bust that cooler up!" Cyril was providing the expensive cooler. Rico gave him a thumbs up and a smile. They also loaded up plenty of fresh water. Willy tossed in a shovel and a four pack of toilet paper.

"Can't go without. " as he held up the bag of paper before tossing it. Bishop added a large folding table.

Johnny looked at Danny "What are you bringing Dan?"

"Enough of these to last us the whole time we are there." Dan smiled as he placed several boxes of cigars into Johnny's trunk. They were sure that they would forget something, but what that was would wait until they needed it.

Hannon lead the way, with Ross, Bishop and Willy. Johnny's car followed behind. Rico sitting"shotgun", with Danny and Tex in the backseat. They went South on the old "Bloody Bayshore Freeway. The Bayshore was a very dangerous road that went along the South part of the Bay. It was two lanes divided only by a yellow line. Many drivers used the middle lanes to often pass cars. They would also cross traffic to make u turns or to get off on the other side. Eventually they would add a cement divider. Hannon and Johnny took their time driving South past the towns of daily City, San Bruno, Millbrea and Burlingame and taking the Highway 92 exit in San Mateo. This would take them up into the small mountain range where they would find the small lake that would be home for a couple of days.

After arriving at Horseshoe Lake, they drove around the area scouting out the best place to camp. They found a spot close to a small river leading into the lake. They both backed their cars and trailers into an area where they could easily unload all of their stuff.

The area they picked out was walking distance from the lake and right along the river that fed the lake. The tall pine trees provided shade from the eighty degree heat that they were not used too being in. The trees also added an aroma that they just were not used to smelling either. There was plenty of room on the ground to set up a camp with a large table, some chairs and places to have several camp fires. The light that showed through the trees gave the soon to be camp ground a pleasant and soothing look and feel.

Hannon and Ross took the axes and saw and headed off into the wooded area to collect wood. Bishop and Willy started to collect enough big rocks that they placed in three circles for the camp fires. Turnbull, Rico, Tex and Danny unloaded the keg and cooler. They found a place next to the river where they would eventually put the keg in. The river was freezing cold from the snow run off. Of course they had to tap the keg and taste the cold beer.

"Ah, just right. It didn't get shaken up too bad. Hannon did a nice job of keeping a smooth ride." Rico poured each a cup of beer.

"Cheers boys!" Tex held out his cup and the four of them touched cups and chugged the beer down.

Hannon, Ross, Willy and Bish stacked up all of the wood and built the fire but didn't light it. They also took the oil lamps out of the trunks and filled them for when the sun went down.  They too had to have a beer or two.

Next they had to get the car ready for sleeping. Johnny unloaded two seventy pound bails of two stringed hay out from under the tarp in his trailer. The boys learned from the rodeo guys that sleeping on hay made the ground soft and kept it from getting wet from the morning do. They would throw down their sleeping bags on top of the hay. They opened all four doors and put a tarp over the doors to form a tent on both sides of the car. The hay , one bail for each side of the car, and sleeping bags were between the open front and back doors.

They unloaded the big table that Bish had and placed all of the twelve bottles of whiskey and tequila under it. They also placed all of the food, which was in coolers under the table too. They finally were ready.

They grabbed their fishing gear out of the trucks of the two cars.

"We still have plenty of light left. Let's get these lines wet!" Willy began to tie his hook onto his two pound test line.

"Contest" Tex shouted "First catch is a winner"

Rico added "Longest wins too"

"And the most caught" Hannon added

With a one of Danny's cigars hanging out of the side of his mouth, Bish asked "Is that just for now or for the whole weekend?"

"Each day" Added Rico.

"Before we go" Johnny pointed to the keg "We need to have a few to start this off right."

And a few they had. Some more than others. They left single file in two lines. One upstream, one down stream.

It wasn't long before Rico got a tug and reeled in a 12 inch trout.

Holding up the wiggling trout " First landed!"

Johnny was struggling with the whole process. He kept breaking his line. It took him for ever to tie his hook. He also kept losing the bait. It would take him forever to open up the little jar with the salmon eggs in it and place them on the hook. Eventually, he just placed a small hand full in his mouth and when he needed one, he just pulled it out of his mouth. That first night, Johnny didn't catch a fish. Probably because he was one of the boys who had more beers than they others.

That first afternoon of fishing saw Hannon catch the longest. A nice 20 inch brown. Tex had the most with four . Ross caught two 19 inch fish, Bish landed one fat 15 inch brown. Rico added one more small trout, Danny and Willy were the last to get back to camp. They were really hopeful of winning some thing. They each walked into camp with three average size trout on their stringers.

They quickly started the fires and Tex set up the two horseshoe pits.

While the fires were getting right the horseshoe games began. They made up two man teams and played to twenty one. Each player had to drink a beer while the game was going on and the losers had to chug a beer. Johnny and Danny were one team, Rico and Tex, Bish and Willy and finally Hannon and Ross teamed up. If they were not playing they were getting dinner ready.

Rico and Tex finished the night undefeated. They beat everyone twice!

"Hey Tex! We should probably let someone else play!" Rico yelled cross the pit to Tex.

"No shit Rico! There isn't any competition around here." He laughed pretty hard and loud.

Almost all of the others, with the exception of Willy, all picked up a rock or stick and tossed it at them. Then they held up their middle finger at Rico and Tex. They all laughed.

With three fires going, they managed to get dinner ready. The hangers that Johnny brought were cooked on skillets. The potatoes had been cut up into small  squares and the ears of corn that Danny had, were boiled in a rather large pot.

They sat around the table in chairs and on some rather large wood stumps and talked about things.

" I ran into the boys from the doc's and Harry Bridges at O'Doul's last week." Johnny said after a pull form his beer and a somewhat half full mouth of the beef from the hanger.

"What's going on?" Hannon asked.

Shaking is head Johnny went on" They are trying to put Harry into jail for being a communist! Can you believe that Shit?" Johnny was getting a little fired up. He had become friends with Harry as well as many of the working class men of the town. When Johnny got mad, his face would turn red and along with the beer and being upset, his face was red.

"Must be the City big shots down town. Mayor, D.A ect." Hannon had a somewhat pulse on the working of the City government.

"I think you are right." But that won't stop him from continuing to do his work." Johnny added that "He and the boys on the docs are going to strike again. They want insurance benefits, you know for medical stuff."

"That will help all of us, for sure." Rico then stood up and walked over to an unopened half gallon of whiskey and opened it up. He took a rather big swig from it and passed it to Ross. When it got to Johnny he held up a hand.

"Not for me! I think that there ta kill ya will." Johnny opened up the first half gallon of tequila and took a short pull and shivered. "Ah that's good stuff."

As they cleared the table and put a match to the oil lamps for the card game, they continued to talk about the labor movement in the City and the gossip at their places of work.

"I'll play for almost anything but not for nothing! Anti up my friend. Twenty five cents!" Bish pointed at the center of the table. Tex tossed a quarter into the middle.

"Jacks or better. Trips to win. Progressive."

Tex began to deal the cards. They had been playing the different poker games for about two hours after dinner was finished and the dishes cleaned up. It was a low stakes game for fun. Penny, nickle,dime and quarters. Three bump limit on raises. First to fold drinks. A shot of whiskey,a shot of tequila or chug a beer was the price to pay for not staying in. The cigar smoke was thick and so was the laughter and B.S.

"Everyone in?" Tex looked around

"I'm out!" Ross took the half gallon of whiskey and poured it into a shot glass.

"Not much luck so far" as he downed the shot. "Ya'd think it would get easier after the thrird/fourth time"

No one had Jacks or better, so Tex dealt out a new set of hands.

Hannon started the betting with"I got a dime" Bish added "Bump it a dime !"

"Twenty to you Johnny"
"Not going to happen. Jimmy, I got worse luck than you. Still haven't won a hand."

Johnny got up and grabbed a couple of the trout and tossed them in a pan of butter and placed it on the fire.

"Anyone else interested in a snack?"Rico  answered with "You bet. Toss that little guy on. You know, the first one caught." Rico was going to make sure everyone knew he won that bet.

Johnny sat out several hands while he fried up the trout and downed several shots of tequila. As the evening moved on the boys continued to drink quite a bit. Johnny was probably the worst off. He staggered away from the fire with the small trout on a paper plate and handed it to Rico along with a fork and a knife.

"Here ya go Rico"

Johnny returned to the fire to set himself up with another small trout that was fried in butter with salt and some pepper. He added some sauce that was lying around  for some reason bit the head of the fish off and spit it into the fire. The rest of the boys were watching as he did it. They looked at each other and laughed. Johnny smiled and ate his fish.

The next morning started with everyone but Willy, a little

hung over. Tex got the bacon and eggs going on one fire and Rico and Danny frying up more fish. Hannon and Ross went out to find and  cut some more wood for the day and nights fire.

Bish was returning from the area set aside for re leaf.

"Good morning boys! I feel much better. Johnny.... you don't look to good."

Johnny was last one to get up that morning as he walked past Bish to go re-leave himself .

He muttered "Yeah .. Yeah ...Yeah"

It wasn't long before the horseshoe games started. And just like the day before, Rico and Tex kept winning. By ten in the morning ole' Johnny had lost ten matches. That was ten chugs and ten beers. After he poured his beer to chug, The keg ran dry.

"Looks like we are out of the beer boys. Going to the hard stuff!" After his chug along with Danny, his teammate, he took apart the gravity flow pump and washed it in the cold river water. He also took some time to splash his face. He was hopeful that this would sober him up a little.

"We got any coffee brewing?" Johnny walked to the fire and found the  coffee pot and poured him self a cup.

With breakfast done and several rounds of "Shoes" played, they all grabbed their fishing gear and went separate ways. Hannon, Ross, Willy and Danny made their way to the lake and found some deep holes that they could fish. Bish, Rico and Tex Worked their way up stream where most of the fish were caught the day before. Johnny sat around the fire and drank coffee for awhile. He eventually worked his way down stream to see if he could at least catch one fish.

For some reason the fish were biting and they all caught their limits. Even Johnny caught several medium size trout, but didn't limit out. Rico kept throwing back the small fish he was catching, hoping for the real big one. Danny was the big winner. He landed a real nice twenty four inch lake trout out of a deep hole that he found. He had to walk a ways to find it, but..

"It ways well worth the walk boys!" as he walked into the camp last again.

By now they were a little hungry , so they had some lunch .

"Keg toss!" Tex bellowed out. He had cleared some ground away from everything and placed the keg on the ground.

"I'll go first." Tex grabbed the keg at each end and whirled around several times like a guy throwing a discus before letting it go.

Each "Boy" took turns "Throwing " the keg. They each used a different technique. It provided some laughs while they also took turns at the whiskey bottle. When it was all said and done, Ross, with his long arms was the surprise winner.

"That's a chug Jimmy! Rico passed him the bottle.

"But I won!"

"Quit your bitch'en and drink"

"Thanks Rico!" `

After a drink or two the boys hit the river and lake one more time.

" Probably won't get a chance to do this for a while. Might as well hit it one more time." Hannon grabbed his gear and took off towards the lake.

"Danny! Where was that hole again?"

Danny quickly grabbed his gear and took off running.

The boys got back one by one with Danny again being last. Hannon and Ross got the fires started and Bishop took care of the oil lamps. Rico and Johnny started the hamburger dinner. They tossed in some potatoes, onions, vegetables, fish and anything else they had in the big pot to make a big stew. They did save the bacon and eggs for the morning breakfast. Coffee was brewing on one fire. The table was set up for dinner.

As they were sitting around the table Rico started the conversation " What is your guys take on what is going on in Europe?"

"Hitler and his Third Reich are making things difficult on FDR. He doesn't want us in another war , but I bet in a year from now we will all be gearing up for something some where. Maybe I'll get to see my homeland of Ireland!"  Hannon wasn't smiling but he did down a shot of whiskey.

"I'll fit right in if I have to go some where in Italy!"

"Shit Rico, you might find a wife" Johnny laughed

"My fat ass won't fit in any fox holes. I'll have to join the Navy!"

"Tex, you'd make a good cook!" Bishop laughed "They'd all call you Cookie"

Tex flashed his middle finger as he finished of a mouth full of the stew.

"Deal the cards!" Ross grumbled. "We can eat and play at the same time."

The night continued on much the same as the previous night. The conversations continued to be about the possibility of war not only in Europe but in the Pacific and a conflict with Japan.

Johnny again ran out of money! "Dam. Thank God this isn't for a lot of money. I'm done for the night boys."

" Last night you ate a moth for a dollar. How much for this?" Bishop held up a nasty looking bug that was held up with the help of a tooth pick. The boys all started to laugh, not thinking Johnny would go for it.

"A buck a piece boys and I'll eat it all." Johnny was feeling no pain.

" No way!" Rico stood up. "Yep! Lets see the money boys." One buy one they each put a dollar on the table.

"You'll probably get this back, but it will keep me in the game for a while."

Johnny poured two shots of tequila. He chugged the first one and followed it with the bug. It crunched as he chewed it. Some of the boys had to turn their heads in disbelief . It was so quiet they could here the crunching. Willy almost threw up. Johnny quickly chugged the second shot , shook his head  and grabbed the cards.
While tossing a quarter in the middle  and a cigar in his mouth he said:

" Seven cards. Low hole card is wild, roll your own. Start with three." Out the cards went.

The game continued on through the night.

The next morning, it took a while after eating to clean things up. They wanted to leave the place clean and looking better than when they got there. They returned to DeNikes and unloaded the cars and trailers. The had half a bottle of whiskey left and a full bottle of tequila.

"Nice job boys." Johnny held both up .

# CHAPTER EIGHT
## TIME TO RODEO

Mother's day for John and Ma was always a special day for them. Even though she wasn't his paternal mother, she had raised and loved him as her own. They had a very special bond between them.

Before Mass on this Mothers Day, John got up early and made breakfast for Ma.. She was a simple woman with simple tastes, but this morning she would have all of the things that she really would like. They were especially good because she didn't have to prepare them! First, fresh squeezed orange juice. A whole pitcher full. Hot coffee, with cream, sugar and cinnamon. Pancakes with blueberries mixed in, with whipped cream. Eggs over easy and all of the bacon the two of them could eat!

The food alone was a treat. Add to that the aroma of the freshly brewed coffee,along with the fried bacon and the just baking bread still in the oven, the house just came alive. Aunt Lizzy loved her roses with the blooming flowers and the different smells that they presented, but the coffee and pancakes brought back memories of her late husband Edward, and when they were first married.

"John, you don't know how much I really appreciate this!" A big sweet smile lit up her face.

"The only problem will be trying to stay awake during Father William's sermon." She started to laugh as did Johnny.

"Its not the food Ma! Its Fathers William. Sometimes, ah.. most of the time, he rambles on and he forgets where he's at!"

Later in the afternoon, the people of Butchertown always put on a small Rodeo at "the Corral"for the Mothers of the area. Some of the best beef was donated by James Allens for the big BBQ. Plenty of vegetables, different kinds of salads and dishes from all of the different ethnic families, made this a great celebration.

Many little kids running around playing games that they love to play, created a pleasant noise and lots of excitement. The open pit that the men took turns turning the sides of beef, put out a steady stream of smoke. The sauce that was continually sprayed on the beef, filled the air with that special Bar B Que smell.

The Rodeo that was going on, was kind of watched, but most families and friends used the time to catch up on the local gossip and sometimes what was going on around the City and the country.

The final event was a mixed horse relay. Teams had to have two men and two women with only two horses. This year, Johnny finally talked Nellie into letting him ride in the race. It was the only event that everyone watched and it was a great conclusion of the Rodeo that lead into finally eating!

After the race, which Nellie's team won again

"Ya know Johnny, there is a rodeo in Redding in two weeks. I'm bringing Brew and Scampers. You could use Brew if you wanted too, to bulldog. You could also ride with our team in the relay race. We need another rider."

Johnny smiled and thought for a quick second

"Count me in. I've wanted to start competing. That would be great! Thanks. I'm sure Rico, Tex, and Danny would love to come along."

Nellie rolled her eyes and smiled

"Sure, that would be fun."

Johnny could sometimes be clueless about certain matters.

"Maybe he'll figure it out someday" she thought to herself.

Johnny and "the boys" would need a ride to Redding. It was a couple of hours north of San Francisco.. He had been saving his money for awhile as he had picked up a weekend job delivering newspapers to the stands on Saturday and Sunday mornings. He could easily get someone to substitute for him. Red Stevens owed him. He had also picked up an extra shift on Monday and Friday driving for Allens south to San Bruno, to deliver to the little towns only butcher shop.

Johnny had his eye on a used machine that was for sale. It was a black 1932 Ford sedan. It had a V- eight engine, eight windows and four doors. It also had  three gears forward and one for reverse. The fifteen gallon gas tank would be able to keep him on the road for awhile. The nineteen cents a gallon for gas was a little spendy, but he could afford it. So he bought it!

With the "new" Ford gassed and ready to go, the four guys loaded up and left for Redding Friday night when Johnny got back from his delivery south.

"Where are we going to sleep tonight?" Danny was curious.

"We'll head to the rodeo grounds, and see! I hear there is usually places in the barns with the horses."

Johnny said as they crossed the bay on the last Ferry of the night to Oakland.

Rico chipped in "We can always sleep in the car or right next to it."

As would have it, the four young men really didn't plan for a lot of things. This being there first rodeo, would be interesting and new. They would begin to experience some fun times and some not so fun.

Waking up the next morning at the rodeo grounds in the car, they felt stiff. With the windows down, it didn't smell to good. Things outside the car were pretty busy and they had to wake up fast.

"You guys should find some breakfast and coffee. I need to

find Nellie and figure out how and where to enter."

Johnny called out to his friends as he relieved himself standing behind an open front car door.

"Sounds good"

Rico said back to Johnny as he was doing the same thing only behind the rear door.

"We'll grab you something too!"

It was a hectic morning for everyone. Saturdays usually were. The guys finally meet up again at the main grandstand. Johnny had paid his entry fee, and they worked there way into the stands to watch the goings on. Nellie had entered them in the team relay race at the end as well as entering herself in the barrel race and team roping event with her father, who drove her and the horses to Redding Friday morning.

Johnny was the first one to compete. Bull dogging started at 1:00 on the west end of the open field. Rico, LeRoy, and Danny sat and watched as Nellie rode Scampers and Johnny was on Brew. It was very hot and dusty by the time they got started. With no wind and no clouds, that 85 degrees seemed like 100 .

As the two horses broke from behind the starting rope chasing the rather large steer, Johnny held on with both hands on the leather reins. It wasn't long before his hat flew off of his head as he prepared to dismount and hug the steer. Once on the animal, he smacked his forehead on something, dug his feet in the dirt to slow the smelly beast enough to try and turn it to the ground. This monster wasn't going to go easy.. After a battle that seemed for ever, Johnny finally secured an over and under hold on the head and neck and got the dirty steer off its four feet.

Nellie rode over to him and tossed him his cowboy hat.

"Not bad for the first time partner. You got one more ride!" Johnny brushed himself off with his hat in one hand

"I think I'm in one piece." He laughed

Out of twenty plus riders that day, Johnny finished in the top ten, but out of the money.

"Looks like we'll be sleeping in the barn tonight men."

Johnny was going to rent a room at a local hotel for everyone if he won some money.

"Lets go get some dinner." Kenny was hungry after the long day.

After finishing there dinner at "The Round Up" diner on Main Street in Redding, they looked at each other when the bill came. Together they didn't have enough money between them to pay the bill.

"What are we going to do guys? I don't want to wash dishes." Danny was concerned

Johnny was pissed that he didn't ask the guys about money before they sat down. They apparently thought he was paying.

"I'll go into the restroom and out the window. Rico give me 10-15 seconds and follow me. We'll pull the machine around front. Tex, you give Rico about a minute and walk out the front door. Dan, give Tex about a ten second lead. Toss some change on the table, you got some change don't you? Dan shook his head yes. Toss it on the table and grab the bill just like you are going to pay it. Walk slow, both of you guys. The back doors to the machine will be open. Jump in!"

Because of the rather large crowd, LeRoy and Dan went unnoticed and things worked out just fine.

"Next time guys, we have to bring enough cash to pay for stuff. We ain't doing this again. I hope we have enough money for gas to get home." Johnny wasn't very happy.

Later that night in the barn, several men from the rodeo put together a square ring made up of hay bales stacked two high.

"What's going on? Rico asked the guy who seemed to be giving out directions and orders.

"Hay fights partner. The guy spit some ugly brown chew at Rico's feet.

"But only for those who are in the Rodeo. You in it? You want to fight?

Rico responded "Ah no thanks. My friend over there may want to. Do you pay the fighters?"

"Yep! Five dollars to fight, if he can make it passed the second round. An extra fifteen for the winner."

"Hey Turnbull" Rico had walked over to him.

"Five bucks if you can make two rounds and fifteen if you win. We need gas money!"

'What?" Johnny questioned Rico

"I talked to that guy there with the handle bar mustache. We do need the money!"

"Sure. Why not. I'd like to make it home. I'll go talk with the guy."

Every Saturday night after the days rodeo was over, the men gathered in the back barn or arena and had somewhat friendly bare knuckle fights. This kept them out of the bars and taverns fighting the locals. Which usually ended up with them in jail and maybe missing the events the next day. They had a match maker and guys bet on who would win. The match maker gave odds and took so much per bet to pay the fighters. He also sold beer in bottles and usually made some good cash.

"All right kid. I need new meat. You'll be in the second fight. You better get ready. You ever do this ?'

"Not like this!"

"Well your awful thin! I'm not sure you'll last the two rounds. Good luck partner."

While getting ready, Johnny overheard the match maker talking to his opponent.

"You got a young skinny kid. Should be easy money for ya. Take him out before the second round ends so I don't have to pay him."

Johnny may have been skinny looking. He was now a good six feet two. He wore very loose fitting shirts because he hated the tight feeling. His pants were also baggy. Only the two inch leather belt around his waste was tight. The muscled 180 pounds under his clothing was well hidden.

"Tex. See if you can get some good odds on me. You know, never fought before,skinny. Make shit up. They think I'll be an early loser. " Johnny reached in his pocket and gave him his last two bucks.

"This is all I've got left, so if you guys can chip in, we could make some good money. I'll make the two rounds for sure."

The first fight went three rounds. It was a brutal fight. Both fighters could barley make it through the first two rounds because they were in horrible shape.

"You learn anything from that fight Turnbull?" Rico asked

"Ya, I better make my punches count."

Turnbull's opponent wasn't as tall as him, but a lot older and heavier. He looked as though he'd done this many times. Both fighters took there shirts off before they got started. Standing in Levi blue jeans and cowboy boots they both touched fists and took a step back.

Johnny's opponent spit in his hands, rubbed them together, smiled and said "Good luck kid."

This older guy had big shoulders that supported his large forearms and meaty fists. He also carried a rather large amount of belly fat that jiggled a little! Johnny, on the other hand, had well defined muscles. His stomach area was flat and showed his "eight pack".

Turnbull took some jabs off  the top of his head and some punches off of his arms as he circled back and forth. He used some jabs of his own, just to see how this guy defended himself. Not much happened that first round.

"Tex. You get some good odds on me?" Johnny looked at LeRoy over the two hay bales stacked on each other.

"You take him out this round, we cash in!"

The second round didn't take much time. Johnny's opponent wanted this over soon. He came out firing lefts and rights at Turnbull's head to end things. Johnny did a good job of blocking and ducking the flurry. Not only did this guy hold his left hand lower than he should and blocked all punches with it, he was getting tired. Johnny set his feet and jabbed with his left hand knowing that the guy would block it with his left. Not caring if the jab landed, Johnny let go of his right hand at an unprotected chin. It landed pretty good. Fortunately the guy also had his mouth open trying to breath in some air. He stumbled back and Johnny followed up with the same combination. It worked again.

Johnny then faked a right and launched a left right left combination with all three punches on the mark. The last left put the fighter to a knee and dazed. Turnbull then drilled him with his best right hand to his nose and it was over.

Buck, the match maker, paid Johnny the twenty he owed him and Tex another twenty.

"Well kid, you surprised me and everyone else. We'll be in Redding in two weeks. I'll be look-en for you. I'll have some one better for you!"

With a smile on his face Johnny said "You'll have to pay me more than five bucks .... Buck!"

"The boys" sat around and watched the rest of the fights, had a couple of cold beers and found a place in the hay loft to sleep. The next morning they returned to "The Round Up " diner on Main Street, and paid the bill Danny still had from yesterday. After paying for the second breakfast they returned to the Rodeo grounds. Nellie still had her events that they wanted to watch and Johnny had the relay to ride in.

"We need to write down all of the expenses that came our way this weekend. I don't want to have to fight every weekend to pay for things. We got lucky!"

The ride back to "The City" Sunday during the late evening was a long one. Thankfully they had plenty of money for coffee to keep Johnny awake, for gas and dinner. The smell in the car was tolerable, as long as the windows were down. None of them had washed since they went to work on Friday morning. They had eaten some spicy eggs for breakfast and some sausages for lunch that didn't agree with there stomachs. It was funny at first, but got old fast. Eventually, when the sun went down, Turnbull found a grove of oak trees along the road and pulled over. Each took advantage of the chance to relieve themselves.

Two weeks later was the trip to Red Bluff. They were better prepared this time. Fortunately for Johnny, he didn't have to go south to San Bruno on Friday, he instead made the delivery on Thursday. Everyone brought along food for dinner on Friday night and a cook stove for breakfast on Saturday and Sunday mornings. Eggs, bacon and plenty of coffee beans for the mornings. Canned beans were also taken just in case they needed them. The beans could be cooked in the cans. They each took along a plate and utensils to eat with, a frying pan and the coffee pot. They also had stainless steel mugs to drink anything from. A tarp was brought with them that could be used as a tent to sleep under. They also made sure they brought extra clothes to change into, a rag, soap and several buckets for water that they could use to wash up.

This would be a longer trip. Red Bluff is north of Redding by about an hour. It's not as big a rodeo, but it still pays good money. Nellie would also be there riding Scampers in her events and again asked Johnny to join her in the team relay, which they finished third in at Redding.

Everyone made it to Red Bluff early Friday night and sat around Nellie and her fathers camp site outside of the rodeo grounds. Bart, Nellie's father, was a real good guy. He too was in the food processing business. That's what he called it anyway. He had made his money and sold out to James Allen. His building was on Evens Ave at the corner of Mendall. It included a barn and corral that extended to Lane Ave. Allens was going to make it into a pork cutting and storage house. They would use the corral area to hold more animals. Allens original building on Evans Ave was to be remodel also to hold all of the coolers on the first floor and enlarge the kill floor to encompass the entire second floor.. They were getting to be the largest processor and needed more space. Bart was hired by Allens to oversee the renovations in his old building and run the new pork room. He would become Rico's new foreman.

Johnny and the Butchertown Boys as they were now known as,were on there best behavior around Nellie and Bart. Rico was unusually quiet. He wanted to make a good impression on his new boss. Just as the evening was about to end, Bart brought out a bottle of his best whiskey and poured everyone a small shot. Including Nellie.

" Down the hatch folks. Here's to a successful rodeo."

Bart emptied his glass as did Nellie. The guys watched in amazement, then followed suit.

"AHH" Thumping his chest, LeRoy tried to talk.

"That's goood stuff."

"Thanks Mr. Rosenberg" Johnny raised his glass up.

"You boys can just call me Rosey. Except you Landucci!

Laughing he followed with "Just kidding"

Everyone had a great Saturday. Johnny finished in the money bulldogging and Nellie won the barrel racing.

"You boys coming over for dinner tonight?" Nellie asked Johnny

"I'd love to Nellie, but I have a date." Nellie looked very disappointed at Johnny

"Not what you think Nellie. I swear!"

"No need to swear Johnny." Nellie had her hands on her hips.

"At the last rodeo in Redding, I promised a fellow that I'd participate in ... ah, how do I explain what they are?"

Johnny wasn't sure how to tell Nellie he was going to fight.

"Hay fights! Father told me all about them. In fact he watched you at Redding. He won some money on you."

"It helps pay for the trip."

Johnny tried to explain things.

"Well you  go right ahead, but just make sure you guys stop by the camp before you bed down for the night."

"Really?" Johnny smiled

"Yep. I need to know if you'll be able to ride Sunday in the relay."

Things went as planned that night. Johnny got his six bucks for going past two rounds with a tough bronc rider. He also received twenty for  winning in the third round. The boys didn't make much on the odds, but still took Buck for a few dollars.

They all stopped by the camp that evening and Rosey poured everyone several shots. Nellie cleaned out a gash that Johnny had on his left cheek and put some ice on his forehead.

The next two rodeos had pretty much the same results. The group of six got along great and really enjoyed watching all of the events. The only downfall to the weekends was sleeping on the hard ground or in some smelly hay loft.

Johnny's next two fights were a little harder each time, but he still won. He took more punches and looked worse after each fight but the money was better with each fight. The final rodeo of the season would be south of San Francisco in Gilroy California. Buck had told him he would be fighting a bull rider from Corning named Colt Conley. He had never lost a hay fight in his two years.

"Be a great way to end the season with you two in the last fight. Everyone wants to see it. Twenty five just to fight and twenty five to the winner."

Buck was pretty excited.

"I'm going to charge people to watch and make me some cash that night."

Those two weeks flew by. "The boys" had watched this Colt Conley fight several times. He got hit a lot, which was good but he had a crushing left hook that knocked everyone out cold. Colt was built a lot like Johnny, but taller. He was a tough bull rider, and actually a real nice guy. He had shot the shit with the boys and Johnny at all of the rodeos.

Nellie had established herself as the top cowgirl at the events. She won a lot of money but that wasn't as important to her as just winning. She didn't need the money. She also got to spend a lot of time with Johnny. He was always so nice to her, treated her like a lady, even though she didn't always act like one much of the time or dress like one. They laughed a lot together with the Butchertown Boys and her father Rosey.

Saturday at Gilroy was just like the other first days at the rodeos. By now the Butchertown Boys had made many new friends and finally felt like they were part of the cowboy culture. They also dressed the part with ten gallon Stetson hats, button down long sleeve shirts, Levi blue jeans and cowboy boots. LeRoy even started to chew plug tobacco, he didn't like to smoke but chewing was different. He got pretty good at spitting in the brass spittoons at the different taverns and bars. Nellie won her barrel race event with her team roping event coming on Sunday. Johnny finished again in the top ten. His fifth place finish didn't make much money but after the second go round, his body felt pretty good. All day long the cowboys in the arena in the different events talked about that coming nights "hay fights." Who was going to win? Many side bets were made even before the  rodeo events of the day were over.

The hay fights started on time In the crowded back arena.

"The Boys" made bets with Buck getting even odds. They had brought some extra money to bet in hopes of Johnny winning. Only four fights were fought before the last and final fight of the season.

"Remember Rock, circle to your left to stay away from Colts left. Make him hit you with his right."

Tex had watched Colt fight several times. "Keep your right up high when things start to happen."

Both Colt and Johnny touched fists in the middle of the ring to show there respect for each other and things got started.

Turnbull began too find his target easy to hit with either hand. Conley's few punches with his right didn't pack much power and his left jab  was slow and easy to block. About a minute and a half into the match they traded several punches in a flurry when, BANG! Colt caught Johnny on the right side of his head right on the cheek bone with that left hook he had heard about.

The sound  of the fist hitting bone was sickening to LeRoy and Danny. They wanted to throw up.

Things went dark for a second for Johnny as the sweat from his face flew and he stumbled several steps towards the hay bales. He didn't go down!

Colt didn't follow Turnbull as he should have because no one had ever gotten up from his powerful left hook. Using both hands to hold him up along the hay, Johnny turned and got both hands up to protect what he figured was coming and the gained his balance. Colt just stood there amazed, and the crowd was silent before erupting. Johnny shook his head and waved with both hands at Colt as if to say come on. Johnny and Colt traded several punches with Turnbull making sure he circled left until the round was over.

"Holy shit!" Johnny had his eyes back and looked at Rico.

"You haven't been hit like that since old Gilberto got you several years ago." Rico giggled.

Tex yelled at Rico and Johnny because the crowd was so loud. "I told him. Get that right up". Tex gestured by raising his own right. " But No, you won't listen."

"Well he has my attention now Tex."

Johnny took a swig of water and could feel a welt starting to grow on the side of his face. He opened and closed his mouth several times to make sure it still worked.

" Got a shot of whiskey?" Johnny smiled. "I'm good now."

"Keep your teeth tight. Breath out of your nose. And get your right up. He hit you with that left because you left your right down." LeRoy was good at seeing that kind of thing.

The second and third rounds were a lot like the first. Both guys were getting tired. Colt was a real tough guy. He took many punches to the face. His nose was bleeding, as was his mouth. One of Turnbull's punches in the third round knocked one of Conley's teeth flying. Both  fighters were covered in sweat and the dust that stuck to their bodies. At the end of that third round, Colt connected again with a big left that sent Johnny on to the dusty dirt floor.

"Get your ass up" Rico screamed at the top of his lungs.

This time Colt came after Johnny. Somehow Turnbull got to his feet. Colt tried to finish him with another left, but Turnbull blocked it and grabbed on. The round ended. The guys watching were yelling and screaming encouragement to each fighter. It was so loud a person could barley think.  It was a wild , crazy and hot atmosphere.

LeRoy tossed a bucket of water in Johnny's face. "Dam it Tex!'

That pissed Turnbull off. His face began to turn red and his eyes changed.

"just stand there and think, I ain't going to say anything else."

Rico knew that look in Johnny's eyes and what the red face meant. He'd seen it before. The crowd was going wild, thinking that Colt was going to finish things off. Little did they know what Turnbull was thinking.

"I've been thinking too much." Johnny thought "Just go fight this guy . He can't hurt me!"

As Johnny walked to the middle of the ring, LeRoy looked at Rico and said

" You didn't remind him to..." Rico put his hand over Leroy's mouth.

"He ain't going to listen! He knows what he needs to get done! Did you see his eyes?" Rico smiled

"I'm surprised it took him this long."

Throwing all caution to the wind, Turnbull fired a right hand over a surprised and tired Conley's low left hand right to the jaw. Not waiting for a response he let go one of his own left hooks to the side of Colts head and finally Conley went down. Without hesitation, Johnny followed Colt. On both knees and hands to hold him up, Colt had no protection. Johnny pounded him two more times to the face. He wasn't sure if Colt was going to get up, but he was ready if he did. The noise level was so high, everyone was on there feet yelling louder than before. Colt rolled over to his back and smiled. It was over.

Johnny sat down on the closest hay bail as  the boys came over to him all smiling.

"Somebody get me an ice cold beer!"

Colt joined Johnny ,the Butchertown Boys, Nellie and Rosey at the camp fire later that night. Rosey had two bottles of his fine whiskey to drink that night. The cool breeze helped both Colt and Johnny deal with all of the pain from  swollen faces,and puffed up hands. So did the whiskey. Both sported real fat lips, and the next morning would produce black and blue faces. Even though he looked and felt horrible, Colt still had his two go rounds on the bulls on Sunday that he wasn't going to miss.

"Your as tough as old leather Colt" Johnny laughed, so did Colt

"Well, bull ride 'en is what I came here for! It certainty wasn't to get my ass kicked!"

As much as Johnny didn't want to, he road in the team relay. If Colt was tough enough to ride the bulls,Johnny could certainly ride in the relay. He also couldn't disappoint Nellie.

# CHAPTER NINE
## ROLL'EN THE DICE

Sitting around the camp fire that night in August of '35 after the rodeo in Gilroy with Colt, was just plain fun. People always say that there is someone just like you some where, well Johnny and Colt found that some one.

Colt was raised on a horse ranch by a single mother just outside of Corning California. Corning in central California where it is very hot and dusty in the summers. His father passed away from consumption when Colt was three years old. He had a sister that was three years older. He didn't go to school very much because his mother needed him to work the ranch. He also lived with his two older cousins that did all of the hard and heavy work. At six years old

Colt began riding and roping. At ten he started to break horses to sell to people around the town of Corning. They also raised bucking horses to sell to livestock operations that used them at the rodeos. Once Colt turned eleven he stopped going to school to work full time on the ranch. His two older cousins had moved on to other things. At eighteen which was five years ago, he had gotten into the rodeo circuit. He started off as a bronc rider, then he fell in love with riding bulls. He was a good bronc rider but was better at riding bulls. He had been making a good living riding bulls and selling horses with his mother from the ranch.

He didn't enjoy the the fighting very much, but grew up fighting with his older cousins and was pretty good at it. He had been doing the hay fights now for three years and was looking for a way to stop. But having never lost, he was expected to fight each weekend.

That night after his fight with Johnny, he told Johnny that he was actually relieved when Johnny had beat him.

"Remember when I smiled at you from my back? I knew I'd never have to fight again."

"I think you know what I'm talking about!"

John did ! Cyril had always told him "that no matter how tough you think you are, there is always someone tougher". John wasn't really excited to find out who that guy was, but someday he would.

Colt also told John and "the Boys" about some of his adventures rodeo' en and how lucky they were that they could do there thing together. He didn't have friends like them. He told them about how much fun the town of Reno was. He had rodeo'ed there two years ago.

"There is a lot to do at nights in that town! Lots of excitement in all of the gambling casinos. Pretty ladies in the dance halls and booze every where. You can even pay certain women to sleep with you. Well not actually sleep, you know what  I mean." He took a breath and continued

"It's easy to go broke, but it sure can be fun." He had a really big smile on his face.

"You guys have to go there. You'll have a blast"

The Butchertown Boys talked a lot about going to Reno for a weekend adventure next summer. They'd have to save some money, because it sounded spendy. Paying for a room, gas, food and entertainment for three days would be expensive. They would have to plan this out real good.

Colt had told them that the games of chance were played a little different than the way they were played at the rodeo grounds. Craps was way different. First of all, it was played on a big fancy felt table, not on a dirt or cement floor. The casino was always "the House". You could bet on certain numbers and each casino had different odds. Black Jack also had different table rules that changed from casino to casino. Then there was the "one armed bandits !" Slot machines. They could be a ton of fun, but difficult to win at."

After another long week of work, "the boys" gathered at DeNikes Tavern for the usual beers and poker in the back room. Under a large tarp, stuffed in the corner, they found Cyril's crap table. He had used it during prohibition to run late night crap games for some of the City's politicians. Cyril new some guys that  salvaged it from The Monterey Hotel during the quake and fire of 1906.

"Cyril! When are you going to teach us how to play craps?"

Rico asked while shaking a fake pair of dice.

"What for? There isn't anywhere around here to play. And you guys aren't going to start any games here!"

LeRoy chipped in "Reno! We hear there is some real action and fun in Reno."

Turnbull added. " This coming August is the sixteenth National Air Races in Reno. People fly in from around the country just to see it and be apart of it. Heard it was a great time."

"You boys don't need that shit. Stick to the rodeo's. More your kinda people. "

Cyril could just see these four guys getting taken advantage of or getting into trouble of some kind.

"That town has some real bad people. You don't even know how to gamble right. Plus what do you care about airplanes?"

It took several nights and conversations with Cyril, but he finally caved in. These guys were going to go no matter what, so he decided to show them the ropes of gambling. After all, he had been there many times and knew the pitfalls. He also had been around that kind of gambling back in the day when he worked for Johnny's father. He could also steer them to the right places and make sure they stayed out of the houses of ill repute!

Business was always slow on Saturday mornings, so after Johnny made his newspaper deliveries, Cyril and "the boys" began playing craps in the back room.

They had to learn the correct way to "shoot" the dice.

"With your thumb and pointing finger, use a nice arc and let them hit about six inches from the back wall. Same toss every time."

Cyril would demonstrate with his hand following through and leaving it in the air.

"If you can, get as close to the middle of the table, so the dice don't have to travel very far."

"Always keep your hands on the rail and don't reach for the dice or chips until the table help
is done doing there jobs. Look like you've done it before."

Cyril would eventually give them all of the little tips on what to do and what not to do. He also had to explain what all of the markings on the table meant.

"This here is "the Field" bet." He pointed at the box that had the 2, which was circled, the 3,4,9,10,11 and a circled 12.

"Many people like it. I don't. Its a house bet. More ways to lose than win."

He spent great lengths explaining the Don't Pass line and the Pass line. Cyril loved to play the Don't Pass because of the better odds. When he was shooting the dice, he always bet on himself. He would place bet on different numbers and often press his winning roles.

"It takes money to make money." the need to win big was always his goal, so he made sure he had plenty of money.

"Hard way bets I think are sucker bets, but when the dice are hot, I'll cover them."

He also talked about YO bets. That's betting on the 11. Cyril liked it as a come out bet and it payed fifteen to one. Problem was, it is a one roll bet.

"Yell YO eleven! And toss out your one or five dollar chip on the table."
The table help will love it and it creates some excitement.

After several Saturdays of practice shooting the dice and then learning how to make bets with no real money being won or lost, Cyril brought out his set of gambling chips. The red chips were one dollar and the green would represent five dollars. They each counted out fifty dollars worth of fake money in chips. Cyril was the house and acted like the "Stick man" and "the Boys" played for an hour. No one ended up with more than they started with. Danny lost all of his fake chips. Johnny and Rico finished with ten bucks apiece and LeRoy had three dollars. They had fun, it didn't cost them anything and they were learning how to play.

"Each one of you will develop your own style of play. Base it on how much money you are willing to lose! Never bet money you don't have. It's nice when you play with the houses money, but remember, it's really yours !"

"When you are betting with chips, it's not like money. You almost forget it's money. It's easier to toss out a chip than a five dollar bill. You know what I mean? Cyril stated.

"There will also be a ton of distractions, so you need to concentrate. All of the people make for lots of noise, guys smoking and yes free drinks. They are watered down, but enough alcohol to get you feeling good and more willing to bet larger amounts." Cyril wanted to cover as many situations as possible. "And the waitresses. They are real lookers. They can take you mind off of playing. If you are winning a lot, they come by more often to act as a cooler."

John asked "Whats a cooler?

Cyril looked at Johnny and replied " A cooler is hired  by the casino to bring bad luck to the table."

"Really! No way. How does that happen?" Johnny asked

"Casino's have always believed in good and bad luck. That there are just some people that are bad luck."

" What do you do when that person shows up?" Dan was holding a drink in one hand and a cigarette in the other.

"You got two choices" Cyril replied "Keep winning or stop playing."

"As Johnny's dad used to always say "you got to do what you got to do, so you can do what you want to do."

They all laughed.

The Friday after the fourth of July would be there first night at the Hotel Golden in Reno. For twenty bucks a night, they'd have one king size bed, a shower and a toilet. They would be there two nights and drive back on Saturday.

All of "the boys" met at Johnny's house on Galvez at 5:00 Friday morning for breakfast and to load up the Ford. Johnny had gassed the machine up and changed the oil the night before. They were out of the house by 5:30 am. Danny and Tex rode in the back seat with Rico up front. "The boys" always sat this way on the rodeo trips, so nothing new. After crossing the Bay to Oakland on the 6:00 AM Ferry, they hit Highway 80 heading North. They figured about a nine hour drive to Reno. LeRoy and Dan fell asleep, while Johnny and Rico drank some hot black coffee. Johnny had rolled a bunch of cigarettes for the ride and he made sure he had one hanging from his lips on the window side. Mornings in July in the Bay area can be warm, but this day was overcast all the way to Vacaville. They kept the windows up to stay warm. By 10:00 things were getting warm as they approached Sacramento and the hotter valley. By Roseville, Dan and Tex were wide awake and all four started getting excited about getting to Reno.

They pulled over in Colfax to get gas and have lunch. They had just started the climb up into the Tahoe National Forest. It was a great ride. The air just seemed fresh as it blew through the downed windows. It had a pine aroma. The one lane shaded road each way was not very straight. The many turns followed the snow filled rushing white capped Truckee River through the mountains. Several times Tex and Dan had Johnny pull over so that they could get there stomachs right.

"Don't look out the side windows, Look straight ahead or shut your eyes." Rico told Dan and LeRoy as Johnny was laughing and trying to keep the Ford on the road.

They went through the little towns of Gold Run, Alta and Emigrant Gap. They finally made it all the way to the top of the mountain road when they reached Donner Summit. They pulled over to rest, relieve themselves, get there stomachs right and look at the scenery. It was something none of them had ever seen before. The beautiful view down to Donner Lake, the forest of tall evergreens and the different colors of flowers growing wild in the many green pastures had a quieting effect on all of them.

"Before we head to Truckee and Reno, I should add some water to the radiator."

Johnny knew that the long up hill climb on the twisting mountain road could be hard on the engine. Cars at that time were known for overheating on long drives, especially up hills and mountains.

Usually, there were places where drivers could fill up the radiators with water. Drivers had to make sure they left the car engine running or else the engine block would crack. While Johnny was filling the radiator with water, Rico, Dan and Tex over looked the long, wide green valley below the timber line of the surrounding gray and snow topped mountains.

"Johnny you got to look at this!" Rico called out

"Just a second, I'm almost done with the water."

"You don't want to miss this!" Dan as pointing down to the valley below.

"This is as far away from Butchertown as one can imagine." Tex was standing with his hands on both hips, also looking down.

The green grass was blowing in the tiny breeze, giving it the look of a small green ocean. As the grass moved with the winds, the shades of green seemed to change from a darker color to lighter and back again. Different flowers of candy apple red dotted the pasture along with wild  bright red rose bushes. Dozens of yellow flowers that seem as bright as the shun grew throughout the green grass. Purple flowers and white patches of beautiful large bushes added to the scene that seemed to be painted. A tiny river wiggled through the grass field as several black tailed deer drank from it.

"I'll tell ya boys, this is something else. It also shows us that we live in a different world. The crap and bull shit that we live with everyday is all we really know and will always know."

After stretching there legs, taking care of the engine, everyone piled into the car for the downhill part of the drive.

The National Air show that they wanted to attend had been

moved to Cleveland in September. That was probably a good thing. They wouldn't have to be driving around a crowded town with others who didn't know where they were going. When they finally arrived in Reno, They stopped at a gas station to fill up the Ford and make sure the radiator was full of water. This way when they left for home they had a full tank and wouldn't have to stop. Just get in and go home. Rico took care of the gas in Colfax, LeRoy payed for the gas in Reno and Danny would buy it on the way home in Colfax.

Now to find the Hotel Golden and drive around town a little to see where everything was. The Hotel Golden was the largest hotel in Reno at the time with over 400 rooms and four floors. It had two restaurants, one on the top floor for fine dinning and a coffee shop on the bottom floor. The hotel had a large parking lot behind it for those staying there just off of North Virginia Street. It was also two blocks from Center Street. When driving down North Virginia Street you passed under the famous sign that arched across the four lanes that read"Reno, The Biggest Little City in the World". During the day, the street wasn't lite up like it was at night. It was as if it was asleep during the day. At three in the afternoon though, North Virginia was about to wake up and come alive.

The first casino going South was Harrods Club. It was a three story building that had a 90 foot by 45 foot mural painted across its front. The picture of the old west pioneer settlers was high above the main entrance and along the street. It claimed to be "the friendliest club in town"'. Inside it presented a cowboy motif. It had pictures of wagon trains on the walls. Also on the walls were many old rifles, deer heads and a very large stuffed brown bear, its arms raised, with its claws and teeth showing. The walls were covered with barn wood giving it that old feeling. The floor was carpeted with patterns of wagon wheels, and Indian tee pees. The different browns,greens, yellows and reds were very bright.

The main gambling room, called "The Covered Wagon

Room", was anything but dull. Cyril was right.

It was loud, smokey and by seven and eight o'clock, very crowded.. Slot machines lined two of the walls. Penny, nickel, dime and quarter machines played ringing noses when they were played.. Several dollar machines were up front by the door playing load music with flashing lights to attract people. The middle of the room had a section of four crap tables just like Cyril's, eight Black Jack tables and one roulette wheel. The wall across from the slot machines had two bars. One for the waitresses and a rather long bar for the patrons to sit at. Behind both bars was a mirror that went to the ceiling making the room seem twice as large as it really was. It also had a night club called "The Boarding Camp", that was used on Friday and Saturday nights for entertainment and a dancing hall.

Continuing South on Virginia street next to Harold's Club was in order; The Reno Club, The Nevada Club, The Frontier and The Bank. Across the street starting at the big sign were; The Prima Donna, Horseshoe Club, Haney's Loans, The Monarch Cafe, Hertz's Smoke Shop, Taggart's Jewelry and a fashion shoe store. A new hotel called Hotel Riverside was just beginning to be built. It would be a ten story building to compete with Hotel Golden.

Center Street, which was walking distance also from the Hotel Golden, had a different set of clubs.. It included; The Palace Club, The National Club, Coney Island Bar, The Old Brick, The White Coaster and The Waldorf Club. This street did have some gambling, but was more night time entertainment. It reminded people of the old "Barbary Coast" of San Francisco during the late 1800's and before the earthquake.. The dance halls were always crowded with young people and some prostitutes. Every once in awhile famous actors and sports celebrities would be seen parting in Reno. It was an easy train ride for the rich from San Francisco and Los Angeles. Flying into Reno was available, but the flights were very bumpy and scared many of its passengers.

Now that "the boys" had the lay of the streets and what was where, they checked into the Hotel Golden. Their room was at the corner of the North end of the building on the second floor.

"What's this? One bed!" Tex wasn't real happy, he thought they would each have a bed.

"We only need to sleep and shower!"

Johnny yanked the top mattress to the floor.

"Landucci and I have the floor. Dan, you and Tex have the box spring. We'll split the blankets."

Questions?"

Johnny smiled.

"You're a tight son of a bitch Turnbull." Dan pitched in.

"You can go sleep in the car and I can get you your money back if you want!" Knowing full well that they really didn't have a problem.

"Who's showering first? Rico looked around. "OK! It looks like it's me!" Rico hustled into the bathroom.

After everyone was cleaned up and ready to go get some dinner, Johnny pulled out of his bag a bottle of some Kentucky bourbon. He also gave each of "the boys" a five dollar bill.

"Compliments of Cyril."

"Dam good man, that Cyril." Tex said, as he was reaching for four glasses from the sink in the bathroom.

"To Cyril" Danny had done the honors of pouring the bourbon.

"To Cyril" they all replied and took a drink.

"One more." Turnbull choked out.

"To Cyril" They all, had one more chance to down a pour after holding there glasses high and toasting.

They each took half of there money that they had brought up with them and put it in a safe place in the room. This way they would for sure have more for the next night.

The dinner at the coffee shop was quick and filling. Out the front door they went to begin there adventure going North on Virginia Street. Wanting to check all of the casinos out before settling on one place to gamble, they took there time walking through each one. They were all different. Some just had slots, some just had Black jack, but Harold's Club had everything.

"I think this is the place boys." Johnny along with the others agreed with Rico.

They were like kids in Moody's Ice Cream Parlor for the first time back in Butchertown. They really didn't know where to start, so they found four slot machines that were all in a row along the back wall that no one was sitting at. They were nickel slot machines. A nice looking gal dressed in a green outfit and cowboy hat came up to them and asked if they needed change. They each gave her a dollar bill for a roll of nickels.

"Don't spend them all in one place boys." she smiled.

LeRoy still feeling the effects of the two shots of bourbon asked.

"Got any drinks?"

"Sure, I'll send someone over to you guys."

It wasn't long before a cocktail waitress with long black hair and a low cut short dress approached them. In her early twenties, with a pretty smile and too much make up, she took there orders for four whiskeys , up. They knew that they couldn't water down straight whiskey.

After about an hour or so on the slots and a couple of those non watered down whiskeys, they made their way over to the Black Jack tables. Not being enough room for all of them at one table, they each sat at different tables. Each being a little nervous, they got right into it. The tables were all at a  one dollar minimum bet. Johnny was playing with a mixed group of older men. Once he got comfortable, he pulled out one of his pre rolled cigarettes and lite it up. Several others were smoking, so it wasn't a big deal. Tex had a big chew in his mouth as he played and Danny had bought a ten cent cigar that he had in his mouth, but wasn't smoking it. Rico had several ladies at his table along with two gentlemen as he sat at the corner to the right of the dealer.

Harold's  dealers, some women, were very friendly. They encouraged conversations among the players. Knowing each others names and where they were from made it much more fun. Enjoying when the dealer went bust made everyone a winner!

"The boys" were holding there own at the tables. They would get behind in money and then catch a black jack or double down on a ten or eleven and win. At Rico's table, Erda the dealer, asked a new player to cut the new deck of cards. He had just laid a fifty dollar bill down to bet and didn't asked for any change. Sitting at "third base" Rico became a little more nervous. His position as the last player was to take or not take cards. Many times it decided who won or lost.. The conversations stopped with such a big bet being played every hand. They went through several decks and hands, when three rather large men dressed in green suits that the security guards wore, stood behind the man with all of the fifty's.

"Sir!" The biggest of the three had a deep voice as he placed his rather large hand on the man's shoulder.

"You need to come with us. Now!"

The remaining two Harold's workers grabbed him under his arms and lifted him off his chair. He started to struggle, but it wasn't going to help. The four men, three in green suits, disappeared through some doors behind the waitress bar.

One of the girls playing at the table asked Erda.

"What's up with all of that?"

"Fake Bills!" Erda smiled

"What's going to happen to him?" The little blonde girl asked.

"The Police will eventually arrive. You'll see him leave with the Police after our boys "Talk" to him for awhile. He won't be looking to good and he might not even be walking!"

Play soon continued on with out missing a beat.

Finally "the boys" found their way to a Crap table all together. They began to follow Cyril's advice of playing the Don't Pass line. The table was "cold", no one had made a point. They had done well as the dice had made there way around the table. Eventually they came to Tex. With big smiles on there faces they each placed a five dollar bet on the Pass Line. Even though it was a one dollar minimum table, they went with the larger bet.

"Hey big boy! Change the luck of the table and make a point!" Johnny yelled out.

"Dollar YO! LeRoy yelled and tossed a dollar chip out.

LeRoy had grabbed the dice just like Cyril showed "the boys". He tossed 'em high with an arc and a big follow through with his right hand.

"Seven! A winner." LeRoy lost his Yo bet, but everyone on the Pass Line won.

LeRoy next threw a nine. Rico, Tex and Turnbull all placed bets on the six and eight. Danny through down four dollars.

"Cover the hard ways please."

The stick man passed the dice to Tex, who being excited, pitched the dice too high and too long.

"Hippy Hop Over the Top" Called out the croupier.

"Try to keep 'em on the table cowboy."

Play continued for several hours with all of "the boys" getting a chance to throw "Dem Bones."

The winnings came with some big loses as the night progressed. At Midnight, they took there chips to the "Cash" window. After all of that time gambling, they each had more money than when they started with.

"You know, If would have bet the Don't Pass the whole time, I would have won a lot more money!" Johnny chuckled.

Rico looked at Johnny "Yep. Sure would have, but you wouldn't had as much fun as we did."

"Hey! Lets see what Center Street has to offer at this time of night. " Dan was excited to see the rest of Reno.

The two street block walk in the late night air was refreshing after being in the stuffy smoke filled Harold's Club.

"Nothing like summer nights. Just makes you want to do something fun." Johnny loved the night air especially at the higher elevation of Reno.

"It smells different up here."

"Johnny, you're right about that! It sure doesn't smell like Butchertown! Tex agreed and they all laughed .

"The boys' walked to the corner of Center Street where the Palace Club was located. It had three entrances. One down Fifth Street, one down Center Street and one big one right on the corner of Center and Fifth. As you looked down Center Street, you could see nothing but bright lights of many different colors. Some blinking and flashing, some not. It was definitely a sight to see. The Palace was just as bright inside as it was  outside. It had some slot machines along a couple of  walls and a big wooden dance floor in the middle. The circular shaped floor was surrounded by tables and chairs, and lots of young people sitting in them talking or on the dance floor dancing. The music was very loud but didn't drowned out the laughing and other sounds that people make when partying.

After dancing, drinking and talking with a group of four girls in town from Eugene Oregon, "the boys" made plans to meet them there again the next night. The two groups left together but the girls headed down Fifth as "the boys" watched them get into there hotel. "The boys" then walked back to North Virginia and stopped at the Monarch Cafe for a late bite to eat before ending up at the Hotel Golden.

Waking up the next morning in there room took awhile. They kept the drapes closed so that it would stay dark longer. They slowly showered and got cleaned up before breakfast at the diner on the first floor.

They decided that they would gamble from two until six, get some dinner and and meet the four girls at the Palace by eight. They had had a great time with them that last evening and figured it would be worth trying again.

Before they left for Harold's Club, they finished the bourbon that Cyril had given them and then walked into  Harold's feeling pretty good and they had enough money to gamble with.

They also decided that they would take that five bucks Cyril gave them and put it on the roulette table. They all chose red and won. They let it ride and it went red again!

"It's going to be a great night guys." LeRoy had a big smile as they headed to the Crap tables.

It was like they were the only ones in the casino. The noise wasn't there, so they created there own excitement. They kept there bets low and often all bet the Don't Pass line. It's unusual when the shooter bets the Don't Pass Line.

"Wow. I haven't seen so many guys bet against themselves. Good strategy guys." The croupier smiled as he talked with "the boys". They liked it when people won and the table was hot.

They made some pretty good runs from 3:00 to just after 5:00 and gave most of it back. The table went from just "the boys" to jammed with no room. People were having a great time and loved it when LeRoy was calling out his Yo!
a
"What time is it?" Turnbull asked Tex. The casinos never had clocks on walls, but Tex had a watch on.

"5:30" Tex Replied.

"One last run boys?" Turnbull looked around

"Lets do it! Give me those white bones" Rico had been making points most of the time before crapping out.

On Rico's final throw, a seven out, was just after six. LeRoy had hit several Yo's and Danny had parlayed the hard six twice and the hard four twice! Rico made countless points and "the boys" walked away with a pocket full of chips.

They met the girls at 8:00 at the Palace and were there until midnight. The gentlemen that they were, they walked the four girls back to there hotel before getting a hug and a kiss from each of the girls.

They wanted to be up early for the long ride home. The cooler air in the morning, would help the Ford climb the mountain and not overheat.

The trip home was full of laughter as they replayed the second night at the crap table and the dancing at the Palace. LeRoy even got an address of one of the girls, and was planning on sending her a letter.

They all put in money, as they bought a bottle of expensive red wine for Cyril.

"We had the time of our lives." Johnny told Cyril as he gave him the bottle at Cyril's Tavern.

"Thanks Cyril." "The boys" all said at the same time.

# CHAPTER TEN
## THE BOARDWALK

Winter months always seemed to drag for all of "the Boys". It was a time to work, often times putting in overtime, save there money and hang out at DeNike's Tavern on Friday nights. Some Saturday nights they would venture across the bay to a popular dance club, but not very often.

Johnny started to go to the Native Sons of California Gym at nights after work during the week. He started boxing to help pass the time. He got someone to train him and he spared a lot. With the head gear on, he never got hurt and got a great workout. Driving all day got to be old. Even though he had to unload the meat products, he needed something else.

After his last amateur fight his trainer told him it was time to"hang 'em up". He had not won any of his three three round fights.

"You have some basic problems John". His trainer told him.

"You have short arms, slow hands and no knockout punch!"

He had taken some good beatings in those three matches and decided it was a good idea to stop. He knew that if those fights were in a barn, he would have outlasted those three guys. They don't keep score in those hay fights. He continued to train and spare with anyone. It was at times fun and gave him something to do at nights.

During a rainy Friday April night at DeNike's Tavern, "the Boys" sat at a table in the back corner. They had played some craps for fun in the back room for an hour. They would often take turns being the house and continue to learn the in's and out's of the game.

"OK men! What are we planning on this summer?" Johnny asked.

Rico answered as he looked at John "Are you rodeo 'en this summer? If so, how much and where?"

"I think so." Not sounding real committed.

"Not as much as last summer. It kind a got old on the road and sleeping who knew where. "

Not being all that good of a bulldogger and winning occasionally, it was difficult financially. Fighting was the only way that helped Johnny stay ahead of things and he really understood what Colt had told him around the camp fire. Plus, he wasn't so sure Nellie would still let him use Brew any more. They hadn't be seeing much of each other.

d

"What about the hay fights?" LeRoy asked

"Defiantly not afraid of anyone, in fact the boxing experience has made me better, but I really don't like waking up so sore on Monday mornings after a rodeo. Plus I'm running out of teeth!"

They all laughed. Johnny had lost several teeth from those fights and was planning on getting some fake ones.

"I'll pick and choose who and if I fight. I can easily tell Old Buck No".

"We have to do something this summer!" Dan got up to buy another round of beers.

"We could always head back to Reno!" Rico suggested and then giggled.

Tex agreed but then said. " I hear that the Santa Cruz Boardwalk is a great place. There is way more to do there than Playland at the beach. I know a guy who takes his family there every summer for a week. He rents a cabin and walks to the beach everyday." Tex sounded pretty excited.

n

"I can get a phone number and call about getting a place for us."

After some discussion, they all agreed that Tex would call and reserve a place sometime in August at Santa Cruz.

Another good reason for going to Santa Cruz instead of Reno was the amount of time driving. Reno was at least a nine hour drive! Santa Cruz was around two hours. They would still have to drive through the Santa Cruz Mountains, but that drive was way shorter.

They had heard of the train that would occasionally leave from Third Street early on Saturday mornings to Santa Cruz and return that night. The riders would have seven hours to enjoy the Boardwalk be for the return trip to the City. Southern Pacific Railroad was offering this special trip on June 20th 1937 for only $1.25 round trip.

"Why don't we do that special, just to see if it's a place where we could have fun for several days." Rico asked everyone.

"Great idea my friend." John answered

"You get the tickets and I'm sure we are all in! It's only $1.25 !"

The 20th of June came around and they had a great time. So good, they wanted to stay the night, but didn't have any way home. They meet four girls from Los Angeles that were there for a week. They had a blast drinking rum and dancing with them at the Coconut Grove Ballroom. They slept the entire trip home on the train!

LeRoy made arraignments to rent a cabin on Trinity Street, which was six blocks away from the main entrance to "The Boardwalk". They could walk every day and night and not have to drive. It would cost $100.00 for the seven days in the middle of August. LeRoy made sure they would each have a bed  in the two room cabin. He wasn't going to sleep in the same bed as Danny any more!

Everyone put in for their vacation time and began to make plans for their adventure. They passed the weekends by playing some semi-pro baseball around town. Cyril had began to sponsor and manage an older team that Rico and John played on. He also sponsored a younger team for the Butchertown kids. LeRoy and Danny managed that group. Cyril loved baseball and so did his only son, who now played on the younger team.

With the trip to Santa Cruz being only about three hours, they didn't have to get up at the crack of dawn or worry about catching a ferry to cross the Bay. Santa Cruz was South of San Francisco and West of San Jose. They all got a good nights sleep in their own beds and had breakfast at home before heading over to Johnny's house to load up the old Ford. They could buy all of the food they would need once they got to Santa Cruz. They were told the two room cabin had a kitchen to cook in and an area to eat.

They headed out of Butchertown at ten in the morning. The California State highway heading South was a new four lane road. Two lanes each way with no divider between to separate the North bound and the South bound traffic. They traveled up a steep grade in Visitation Valley called Boneyard Hill that had many accidents because of the no divider in the road. The road straighten out just before passing the towns of Brisbane, South San Francisco, San Bruno, Burlingame, Redwood City and finally into the country and on to San Jose. The drive to San Jose was about 50 miles of beautiful weather. They had to keep the windows down because it so warm. They could smell the different crops that were being grown before getting to San Jose. Mint was the the most noticeable aroma and the long rows of corn seemed like they went on for miles.

They got off of Route 68 South in San Jose and turned onto Highway 17 West through the little town of Los Gatos on the way to the old "Glenwood Highway". This road took them through the Santa Cruz Mountains following along side the train tracks for much of the drive. They stopped in the small town of Glenwood around noon to get some lunch, hit the head and fill up some mugs of coffee.

Turnbull kept the speed down through the one lane mountain road. Danny and LeRoy suffered through the trip to and back from Reno last summer because of weak stomachs. Every once in awhile the road had a passing lane, but they always let other cars pass them. Rico had to hold Johnny's coffee mug, because he was always shifting the three speed engine. Usually he would put the mug between his legs as he shifted, but this road had many turns and it became easier for Rico to hold it. He wasn't doing anything but talking. Johnny couldn't use his left had to smoke because it needed to stay on the steering wheel, so his cigarette just dangled on his lower lip. Some of the new cars on the road had radio's in them but the Ford was too old for that. They didn't need music to entertain them though. The work at Allen's, where Johnny, Rico and Danny worked and Moffatt's where LeRoy worked, provided lots of issues to talk about.

Johnny had continued to be involved in all of the union negotiations. After the strike, things continued to get better for the workers. They had received five paid days of vacation, but everything else was taking time and plenty of effort by both the unions and the companies. They were working on getting some kind of medical insurance, but that would take a long time and probably end up with an other strike.

They also talked a lot about what was going on in Europe. Germany and it's new leader of what was called the Nazi Party, Adolf Hitler,  was causing many problems. Many German Jews were beginning to leave Germany and arrive in America. There was a lot of talk about another World War.

Time went fast as they approached a  sign over the road entering town that read "Santa Cruz" in big letters. "the boys" drove through town and found their way to Trinity Street and the cabin. It had a place to park the old Ford off of the street. The front of the cabin had three wooden steps up to a small porch with a rail and chairs all facing the street. Below the porch, instead of a lawn, was an area of sand all the way to the street. There were no sidewalks. The side of the house where the Ford was parked had a huge bush covered with red and pink flowers. The brown colored cabins front door came with a screen on it that opened into a small open room with a fire place that they would not have to use. A hallway lead to the kitchen and two rooms off to the right side of the house. The bathroom was next to the kitchen and had a shower, toilet and a window that opened to a small yard off the cabin next door.

The kitchen had an old wood stove, ice box, a table with four chairs to eat at and plenty of cupboards to store food. Some of the cupboards had pots, pans, plates,glasses and eating utensils. There was also a stack of wood outside the kitchen door to burn in the wood stove. They also found a Bar-b-Que next to the wood pile. Once they settled in their rooms, that came with two beds a chair and a cabinet to put their cloths in, they opened up all of the windows and doors to create a breeze and refresh the cabin. LeRoy and Johnny took off to the store for food. When they returned, they joined Rico and Danny on the porch ,who were listening to the radio from inside and sipping some bourbon.

"How nice is this?" Rico asked.

"Short drive, great weather and old friends to relax with."

"No complaints here." Tex agreed as he took his place on the porch.

The ocean breeze was so relaxing that ten minutes later, Johnny fell asleep in his chair. The drive and a chance to relax also added to his chance to sleep.

By six that evening the bar-b-q was cooking four rib eye steaks, the stove had several ears of corn boiling and four russet potatoes chopped up and frying in some bacon grease that they brought with them. "The boys" each had a cold Falstaff beer from the ice chest.

"I'm thinking the Great Dipper tonight men." Dan suggested for the evening.

"After his dinner, I'll watch. I'll lose it on some of those loop d loos !" Turnbull stood up and grabbed a beer.

The Great Dipper was right on the East edge of the Boardwalk. It could be see for miles. The wooden roller coaster really was the face of the park.

That first evening they made sure that they played some skee ball, which was becoming one of everyone's favorite games and the rage of the East coast. It had a large wooden ball and plenty of whistles, bells and lights that could mesmerize players. They also rode on the Round-up, tilt-a-wheel and the little motor boat rides. Each ride was ten cents, so they made several trips on each ride.

For ten more cents, they each bought some saltwater taffy from Marini's that they ate while walking around and checking things out. They looked in at the Coconut Grove dance hall, but being Monday night, they gave it a pass and walked back to the cabin.

On the walk back to the cabin at Trinity , "the boys" noticed at the corner of Cliff Street and Second, a two story house that had two older Italian looking men and what looked to be their wives.

"How are you guys doing on this beautiful warm night?" Johnny asked as he waved at the two couples.

They smiled and the older of the two men held up a jug of wine.

Waving back at "the boys" "Come join us."

The four boys looked at each other and climbed the five stairs to the covered porch and joined them for a glass of red wine. They had some good Italian music playing on the phonograph and you could smell the aroma left over from the nights dinner. After introductions and hand shakes they began a nice conversation. The two couples were from San Francisco and vacationing in Santa Cruz for two weeks. The older couple were the parents of the other lady and her husband. Not wanting to over stay the welcome, "the boys" said good night and headed back to their cabin.

Tuesday morning was bacon and eggs for breakfast and lots of black coffee.

"The smell of bacon and coffee! Great way to start the day." Rico said while sitting down at the table.

They all dressed in something to swim in , grabbed towels and two ice chests full of  12 oz cans of Burgie beer. They spent the morning on the main beach enjoying the water and the weather until some dark clouds rolled in. This would be a great time to head into The Plunge. The large building had among other things, an indoor natatorium with a diving pool and large slide. It wasn't as big as the pool at the Cliff House, but was a lot newer.

Not many people were in the pool which was very nice and warm. No little kids at all ! Once the clouds left outside, they all went back out , grabbed some hot dogs at the stand at the entrance to the Boardwalk next to The Plunge and walked back to the cabin. They past the  two story house where they met the two Italian couples but today it was just the older gentleman there sleeping in his chair on the porch.

"The boys" showered up, bar-b-q ed and headed back to the Boardwalk. This night the Coast Guard Reserve band was playing music on the bandstand outside of the Casino Arcade. The music could be heard around the park as "the boys" hit all of the rides including The Funhouse. The Funhouse, for 25 cents, had a turning disc, a shaking tunnel, five slides where you sat on a potato sack all the way down and blowholes on the stairs to the top every where to startle people. It also had different sized mirrors that made people look funny!

After The Funhouse, they all went to the Coconut Grove to check things out. The last two weekends the Grove was entertained by the great Bennie Goodman and also Lionel Hampton. It was one of the most popular spots for all of the Big Bands. The crowds were great and the band members would enjoy the Boardwalk during the days. Friday and Saturday night the famous Tommy Dorsey and his band would be playing. That would bring in a large crowd, so they would have to get there early those nights.

Wednesday at the Boardwalk would be a little different. On the other side of the long wharf, which split Cowells Beach and the Main Beach, were two new opportunities. The first was a speed boat tour. The Miss Stagnaro had seating for eight passengers in two rows at the front of the boat and two rows of three seats at the back and near the three large motors that powered the vessel. The driver and the tour guide sat in the middle. The boat sped along the shoreline North above Cowells Beach, back South around the wharf, past the Main Beach and past the Boardwalk with the Great Dipper. "The boys" each paid fifty cents for the one hour ride after they had spent four hours on a fishing boat just off of the wharf. They each caught several white fish that they packed in ice and would later that night bar-b-q for dinner.

On there way back to Trinity Street, they past the house with the older Italian family. The older gentleman was there. Awake this time and waved them over. They again shared some of his home made wine. Enrique and his wife Celia were in the florist business in the City. Their daughter Agnes, was staying with them and her husband Charlie, who was there that first night, had driven back to the City to work for a few days at his flower shop in the famous Saint Francis Hotel. He would be back on Friday with their two young grand daughters. They had been making this vacation  now for several years.

The two older women who were cooking that nights dinner, were in and out of the conversation on the porch. The aroma of garlic, onions and other herbs, spices and sauces were very pleasant. They asked "the boys" if they wanted to stay for dinner, but as much as they would have liked too, they said no. They had to bar-b-q that mornings catch.

The next two days and nights "the boys" continued their vacation by going to Cowell's Beach on the other side of the wharf. They drink beer and bar- b-q ed   hot dogs that they had brought from Allen's sausage kitchen, right on the beach. The air was very warm and thick with the smell of the saltwater and something they just could not put their finger on. Of course as they walked around the Boardwalk they were surrounded by the ever present smells of cotton candy, saltwater taffy, roasted peanuts and the sounds of laughing children, screams from the Great Dipper, music and noise from the Casino Arcade. They spent some time playing more skee ball at the Arcade which was in the connected building next to The Plunge.

Friday and Saturday nights, The Coconut Grove served exotic cocktails from places like; Hawaii, Cuba, and Brazil. They really were just rum and cokes put in fancy tumblers, garnished with mints, cherry's , little umbrellas and given fancy names. It was a fun atmosphere and added to the excitement. If you drank too many of those fancy drinks, the next morning could be difficult. Friday night was very crowded and they didn't have a place to sit. They did get some good dancing in and at the end meet three young ladies who promised to meet them there on Saturday night.

Saturday, the final day was spent cleaning up the cabin on Trinity Street and emptying the food cabinets. They decided to have an early dinner and get as much cleaning and packing done while they weren't in a hurry. They next morning all they wanted to do was clean up, throw their stuff in the Ford and get breakfast at the little diner called The Surf Club before heading home.

On Saturday night, just as Friday night, Tommy Dorsey and his band were playing at the Coconut Grove. Tommy was known as the "Sentimental Gentleman of Swing". He played a smooth toned trombone and his band was known all around the country. They put on a great show and were always great to dance to live.

The show started at 8:00, so "the boys" left the cabin at 5:30. They walked by the house on the corner of Cliff and Second street and could see that the Italian family was seated at a large table eating dinner.

"I can smell that meal all of the way out here." Rico said

"Smells like my mothers cooking! I just know it tastes great."

"You get to eat that kind a cooking all of the time. Us Texans don't." LeRoy replied as they all kept walking.

"I sure would love to sit at their table for a night."

"OK Tex! I get the hint. I'll have you over for some of Moms good cooking when we get back to the City."

"What about me? Dan asked

"My birthday is coming up, so I'll have all of you guys over. My mother loves cooking for large numbers." Then Rico giggled.

They walked up the ten steps of cement stairs leading into the Boardwalk, just like they had the previous days. The first ride they walked by was the Merry-go-round, then under the large archways in front of the Casino Arcade that faced the  main beach and the Pacific Ocean. For ten cents, people could get their pictures taken in the little photo booth that was under the arches.

"The boys' each bought a bag of peanuts for a nickel to eat before heading into the Grove for the evening.

"We need to find a table that is close to the restrooms." Johnny told the guys.

"Why? Tex asked

"Because every gal in this place is going to go in there at one time or another. We don't want to miss any one cause we are in the wrong spot! " Johnny smiled.

Tommy and his band started right on time. Their first tune was called "The Hawaiian War Chant." It went along with all of the special drinks that were being served and got the crowd in a great mood.

After a half hour or so, Johnny spotted a tall young gal with very black hair pulled up in a very attractive style.

"Rico! Check that out." Johnny never got to excited about ladies, but this one really got his attention.

"Not bad...not bad" Rico agreed

"Not bad? That's all you can say? Come on she's got a friend."

Johnny pulled Rico out of his seat to go ask her to dance, but before they could make their way through the crowd, two sailors dressed in their white uniforms got there first. Waiting impatiently, Johnny walked towards the dance floor as the tune ended. Walking back to her table, this young ladies eyes met up with John's as he asked her to dance. The band began playing "Boogie Woogie"

"Sure" she said. And they danced through the tune. Being taller than most women and in shoes with heels, she was almost eye to eye with Johnny. He had a great smile and there was something about his eyes she liked. When Boogie Woogie ended, Jack Leonard the singer in the band, started in with "Our Love" a much slower tune.

"Would you like to dance one more?" John asked

"I think so." She smiled

This time she could feel his strong arms and had to look up to him. Which she really liked.

Johnny looked down into her dark brown eyes, with thin eyebrows and a really attractive nose. As with the style, the bright red lip stick brought out her perfectly shaped lips. With her hair up, it showed off her neck. The dress she was wearing had padding in the shoulders and gave her a flat look across the back. It was buttoned all the way up to the top and still showed off some great lines as she turned her head. He could almost feel her breath on his neck as they danced very slowly.

"May I walk you back to your table?" Again she smiled

"Yes, I would like that,."

John pulled her chair out as she sat down.

"May I?" pointing at the chair next to her.

She shook her head up and down and flashed her beautiful smile again.

"My name is John Turnbull. May I ask yours?"

"Rose. My name is Rose Angelo. And this is my cousin Marion."

Marion was older looking, but also had black hair and a dark complexion.

They sat and tried to talk, but the music was very load.

"Would you two like to walk outside and sit under the archway?" John would rather talk with just Rose, but didn't want to sound to forward by just asking Rose.

"You two go ahead." Marion said

"I came here to dance." She laughed.

John pulled the chair as Rose got up and he helped her put on her very nice white sweater..

They found a bench to sit on for awhile to talk. They decided to ride the near by Merry-go-round and catch a ring or two.. After the Merry-go-round they walked by "Winnie's Turnover Pies". John bought Rose a pie with some warm apple filling and he had one with huckleberry filling.

"Would you like some buttermilk?" He asked.

Rose laughed and said "No thanks. This is plenty."

How was it?" John asked

"Just fine thanks, and yours?"

"Well, I've never had huckleberry before! It was OK."

They finally settled on a bench by the wishing well in front of the Casino Arcade.

Rose could not believe how easy it was to talk to John about so many things. She felt very at ease talking with this guy she had just met. They had a real good laugh when they found out Rose worked with John's sister Margret at the Bank of America in downtown San Francisco.

"She has been trying to set me up with you for months. Always telling me about her very nice brother."

"And she has told me about this tall pretty Italian girl at work that I should really get to know!"

John looked at Rose and continued "But obviously you know my sister." as he laughed.

"Well, not really. She's not the friendliest person at times and I thought that her brother would be just like her. Thank God you're not!"

As Tommy and the band finished up with their last tune, John and Rose walked back to the table Marion was sitting at. Rico, Tex and Danny were there too.

"These very nice gentlemen were kind enough to join me and not leave me sitting by myself." Marion said as she stood up with her hands on her hips! Then she smiled.

The six of them walked out of the building together.

"Can we walk you guys to where you're staying?" John asked

"I'm sure that would be acceptable." Marion replied

"We are staying just off of Second Street at the corner of Cliff. We are staying with our Aunt and Uncle." Rose followed with.

"Great! That's on our way to Trinity Street." Rico added.

When they arrived at the two story house that the girls pointed out, "the boys" started to look at each other. "Really?" John asked

"Yes, This is it. Why?" Both girls asked.

John explained how they passed by here everyday and had a chance to meet and drink wine with the older couple that was staying there.

"We had no idea, you two were here also. They told us about you two, but we just figured you  were really young. I mean really young." John was gesturing with his arms and hands and pointing at them.

They all laughed and finally "the boys" said good bye and how nice it was to meet the girls. John asked Rose if he could stay and talk with her some more on the porch.

"I'll see you guys in a bit." Johnny waved at "the boys" as they walked away.

John and Rose sat on the porch until the sun began to come up. They had a great talk and exchanged phone numbers. They also made plans to go out together when she got back to the City. They also promised to not tell Margret that they had spent this time together.

John knew it was time to leave, he really didn't want to, but he had too. He wanted to kiss her good bye but he  wanted to be a gentleman and not ruin the trust he thought he had developed with Rose. He stood up, grabbed and squeezed both of her soft hands and looked right into her eyes.

"I'll see you again soon and I'll call you."

Rose returned the squeeze and the look and replied

"You better! I now know how to find you!"

She had hoped he would kiss her, but knew after he left, that he would eventually.

# CHAPTER ELEVEN
## WHAT'S NEXT?

John was pretty excited when he got back to the cabin. The others were still sleeping. He made a final pot of black coffee, showered and packed his things in the Ford. He also opened all of the windows and doors, to help air the place out. Just in case they wanted to come back next year, they wanted to leave the place clean and in good shape.

All "the boys" eventually woke up and did as Johnny had already done. They were laughing and talking the whole time about everything that went on during the week.

"See ya next year Trinity Street cabin. LeRoy waved at the

cabin as he was the last to get into his seat in the back of the car.

The conversations didn't stop at the diner during breakfast. Johnny made sure he got two cups of coffee for the drive and rolled up several cigarettes. He hadn't gotten any sleep, but since he was driving he would need the coffee.

Once they started the drive on Highway 17 east towards San Jose, Rico started the conversation about last night.

"So, Turnbull, tell us all about your new friend."

"I was wondering when one of you knuckleheads was going to bring her up!" Johnny continued to look straight ahead and shift into another gear.

"You sure have a shit eaten grin on your mug." Tex observed.

"What' s her whole name?, where is she from?, will you be seeing her again?" Tex continued.

"What! Are you writing a book?" Johnny knew he would have to tell everything to his friends. He actually wanted to. So, he spent the next twenty minutes in between sips of coffee to talk about his evening with Rose.

Then Dan asked. "What about Nellie?"

Johnny answered "I haven't thought about her! Yeah, well I'll have to figure things out."

He handed his coffee to Rico and down shifted as they went around a corner.

Everyone's life would soon take  a large turn. The war in

Europe was getting worse. America was sending supplies over seas to help with the effort to stop Hitler's  German war machine. December 7th changed what Americans knew as way of life. The Adventures of the Boys from Butchertown would continue. Stay tuned!

# ABOUT THE AUTHOR

The author of The Boy From Butchertown, Steven Turner, actually worked in San Francisco's Butchertown and at James Allen's and Sons's in the 1970's. It was at that time the largest meat packing establishment west of the Mississippi River. Steve did many jobs at the plant including working on the "Kill Floor" and clean up crew. Both of his brothers Bob and Paul also worked there along with their father Bob. This was a summer job for them while they were attending college.

Steven went to Willamette University in Salem Oregon from 1972-1976. During his time at Willamette University , he was a member of the Phi Delta Theta Fraternity and played four seasons of Varsity Football. AS a player, Steve earned All Conference honors three times. After college, Steve Began a teaching and coaching career in Oregon. He taught at the middle school level and as a high school teacher for 36 years and is still coaching football as of 2025. During his football coaching career , his teams won two State Championships and assisted on two more. He coached in over 500 varsity football games.

Steve was married to Mary for over 35 years and they have two sons. Robert is an Officer in The United States Marine Corp and John is a property manager in Oregon.

# ABOUT THE BOOK

Part of San Francisco's pass history includes a section of The City once called "Butchertown". During the late 1800's and early 1900's this section of town along Isias Creek, was home to 24 slaughter houses. The population of this neiborhood was very diverse. Most of the adults immigrated to the United States from many of the European Country's and few spoke English. This group of new Americans worked hard for very little pay. They were tough people and had to fight for what was theirs.

Johnny Turnbull and Ricco Landucci were both born in homes on Galvez Ave the same month in 1915. They began a friendship that lasted their entire lives. They were joined by Tex and a younger Danny Cary. These four traveled through out The City and parts of Northern California. The adventures that these guys had included trips to the beach and playland, playing sandlot baseball, high school football, fishing trips, gambling in Reno, hayfights at rodeos and summers in Santa Cruz. They also fought together against big business on the waterfront during Bloody Thursday during the Strike of 1934. Enjoy their experiences and friendships that became changed on December 7 1941.